Lamb

FROM THE
NANCY DREW FILES

THE CASE: Uncover the conspiracy that has brought the prestigious Face of the Year modeling contest to the brink of disaster.

CONTACT: Nancy's friend Bess is a finalist—but she's in danger of falling victim to the mysterious saboteur.

SUSPECTS: Roger Harlan—*the superhunk model poses with all the girls, but an incriminating piece of evidence links him to the crime.*

Thom Fortner—*he's in charge of publicity, and every "accident" adds up to more stories in the press.*

Heather Richards—*a knock-out contestant who seems determined to knock out of the competition as many of the others as she can.*

COMPLICATIONS: Nancy vows to find out who is behind the conspiracy, but first she has to deal with the threatening note she finds on her pillow: "If you like your face the way it is, keep your nose out of other people's business"!

Lamb

Books in The Nancy Drew Files® Series

#1	SECRETS CAN KILL	#37	LAST DANCE
#2	DEADLY INTENT	#38	THE FINAL SCENE
#3	MURDER ON ICE	#39	THE SUSPECT NEXT DOOR
#4	SMILE AND SAY MURDER		
#5	HIT AND RUN HOLIDAY	#40	SHADOW OF A DOUBT
#6	WHITE WATER TERROR	#41	SOMETHING TO HIDE
#7	DEADLY DOUBLES	#42	THE WRONG CHEMISTRY
#8	TWO POINTS TO MURDER	#43	FALSE IMPRESSIONS
#9	FALSE MOVES	#44	SCENT OF DANGER
#10	BURIED SECRETS	#45	OUT OF BOUNDS
#11	HEART OF DANGER	#46	WIN, PLACE OR DIE
#12	FATAL RANSOM	#47	FLIRTING WITH DANGER
#13	WINGS OF FEAR	#48	A DATE WITH DECEPTION
#14	THIS SIDE OF EVIL	#49	PORTRAIT IN CRIME
#15	TRIAL BY FIRE	#50	DEEP SECRETS
#16	NEVER SAY DIE	#51	A MODEL CRIME
#17	STAY TUNED FOR DANGER	#52	DANGER FOR HIRE
#18	CIRCLE OF EVIL	#53	TRAIL OF LIES
#19	SISTERS IN CRIME	#54	COLD AS ICE
#20	VERY DEADLY YOURS	#55	DON'T LOOK TWICE
#21	RECIPE FOR MURDER	#56	MAKE NO MISTAKE
#22	FATAL ATTRACTION	#57	INTO THIN AIR
#23	SINISTER PARADISE	#58	HOT PURSUIT
#24	TILL DEATH DO US PART	#59	HIGH RISK
#25	RICH AND DANGEROUS	#60	POISON PEN
#26	PLAYING WITH FIRE	#61	SWEET REVENGE
#27	MOST LIKELY TO DIE	#62	EASY MARKS
#28	THE BLACK WIDOW	#63	MIXED SIGNALS
#29	PURE POISON	#64	THE WRONG TRACK
#30	DEATH BY DESIGN	#65	FINAL NOTES
#31	TROUBLE IN TAHITI	#66	TALL, DARK AND DEADLY
#32	HIGH MARKS FOR MALICE		
#33	DANGER IN DISGUISE	#67	NOBODY'S BUSINESS
#34	VANISHING ACT	#68	CROSSCURRENTS
#35	BAD MEDICINE	#69	RUNNING SCARED
#36	OVER THE EDGE	#70	CUTTING EDGE
		#71	HOT TRACKS
		#72	SWISS SECRETS

Available from ARCHWAY Paperbacks

THE
NANCY DREW
FILES™

Case 51
A MODEL CRIME

CAROLYN KEENE

AN ARCHWAY PAPERBACK
Published by POCKET BOOKS
New York   London   Toronto   Sydney   Tokyo   Singapore

AN ARCHWAY PAPERBACK *Original*

An Archway Paperback published by
POCKET BOOKS, a division of Simon & Schuster Inc.
1230 Avenue of the Americas, New York, NY 10020

ISBN: 0-671-70028-6

First Archway Paperback printing September 1990

10 9 8 7 6 5 4

Printed in the U.S.A.

IL 6+

Chapter

One

IMAGINE, NANCY—me, a world-famous model!"
Bess Marvin's lively blue eyes were shining, and
the smile on her face was more than intense. She
ran her fingers through her long blond hair and
struck a nonchalant pose, gazing at herself in the
mirror.

"This is fantastic news, Bess," Nancy Drew
said, rereading the letter that had come for Bess
the day before. "'Dear Bess Marvin,'" she read
aloud. "'We're happy to inform you that you've
been selected as a finalist in the Face of the Year

contest jointly sponsored by Smash Clothing, Elan Modeling Agency, and *Teen Scene* magazine.' It really is incredible," Nancy concluded.

Bess continued to gaze at her reflection in the closet door mirror. "All I did was lose a few pounds, and suddenly my whole life has changed," she said with a happy sigh. "I guess it was worth it to turn down all the ice-cream cones, brownies, mocha cheesecake . . ."

"It's really great," said George Fayne, Bess's cousin and good friend, who was sitting on Bess's bed. "When I took those pictures, I never dreamed they'd actually get you into the finals."

"You didn't?" Bess spun around and faced her cousin. "George Fayne—are you saying I'm not beautiful enough to be a model?"

Nancy held up a hand. "Hold on, Bess," she said. "George just means she's surprised because there was so much competition."

"Right!" George's wide brown eyes were fixed innocently on Bess. "*You* were the one who said over five thousand girls sent in their pictures—"

"And only eight were selected as finalists," Nancy finished for her. "That's pretty amazing."

"It is, isn't it?" Bess said with a sigh.

Nancy brushed back her silky reddish-blond hair and glanced quickly at George. Ever since

2

the letter had arrived, Bess had been subject to some pretty wild mood swings.

Now, for instance, when Bess turned back to the mirror she was biting her lip and frowning.

"Those pictures George took made me look so glamorous. Let's face it, I'm not *that* pretty in real life." She turned from the mirror and flopped down on her bed.

"You are too!" George insisted.

"I agree," Nancy added. "But even if you weren't, there's no sense worrying about real life now. This is a modeling contest! You're going to be treated to an all-expenses-paid trip to Chicago, get a makeover by a professional makeup artist, and have your picture taken by world-famous photographers. It'll be the time of your life!"

Bess nodded, her expression brightening. "You're right!" she said, sitting up. "Besides, the judges aren't only looking for beauty. We'll be judged on personality as well." Bess had no doubts about her personality. "And with you two there, how could I help but be a winner?"

George raised her eyebrows and bit her lip. "Bess, I didn't want to tell you, but I can't go. I'm playing in the All-County Tennis Tournament this week."

Bess winced. "What about you, Nan? You can come, can't you?"

"Better say yes, Nan," George suggested. "Without you there to hold her down, Bess may float off planet Earth."

"I wouldn't miss it for the world," Nancy said with a grin. "In fact, if we're leaving tomorrow, I'd better go home and pack right now!"

"Hurry! Please, sir," Bess sounded truly desperate. She was standing on the sidewalk in front of the Chicago Inter-Continental Hotel with Nancy, waiting while a bellhop loaded their suitcases onto a wheeled luggage carrier.

The elderly man just smiled and hefted the last bag onto the pile. "Ready, ladies?" he said, pushing the cart through the doorway.

Bess stopped short just inside the lobby. "Oh, no!" she shrieked, staring at her hand in horror.

"What's the matter?" Nancy asked.

"Just look at that chip on my fingernail! I was so careful, too!"

Nancy examined the offending nail. It was barely noticeable. "It's tiny, Bess. You can fix it when we get upstairs."

"Oh, no, I can't," Bess moaned. "I didn't bring that shade." She squeezed her eyes shut and

4

shook her head helplessly. "Oh, please, please, let there be a store in Chicago that sells Heavenly Pink. I'll die if I can't find it."

"Gosh, Bess," Nancy ventured. "Is nail polish really worth dying for?"

"I guess I am getting carried away, huh?" she said, apologizing. She hurried across the thick red-and-black carpet to the reception desk.

"Hi, I'm here for the Face of the Year contest," Bess announced to the man behind the desk. He wore a gold pin with his name, Mr. Johnson, on it.

Mr. Johnson peered over the counter at Bess and adjusted his glasses. "Are you one of the contestants?"

"Yes," Bess said, a little annoyed. "I'm Bess Marvin, and this is my friend, Nancy Drew. She's staying with me."

"I only asked because the other contestants have already left for the pier. They're doing a 'Welcome to Chicago' shoot there. It's two blocks north on Lake Shore Drive."

"Oh, no, we're really late! I'm so mad I wasn't ready when you got to my house," Bess said to Nancy.

"Sign here, and I'll have your bags brought to your room. Suite four hundred twelve," Mr. Johnson said calmly. "Good luck."

"Thanks," said Bess, who was running for the glass sliding door.

Nancy followed, and soon the two were dashing up Lake Shore Drive, searching for the other contestants. The scenery was breathtaking, with the skyscrapers of the city towering over the lake. Bess was too nervous and hurried to notice.

"There they are," Nancy announced after only a block and a half. She pointed across the street to a huge pier jutting out into Lake Michigan. A truck with its own electric generator was parked on the pier, and farther out a group of young women were arranged at a railing.

"Great!" Bess said excitedly, stepping off the curb to cross the street.

"Whoa," Nancy said firmly, taking her friend by the arm and pulling her back. "Let's wait for the light."

"Ooh, I can't believe it. There's Kelly Conroy!" Bess whispered excitedly as they stepped onto the pier. She pointed to a young woman with dark auburn hair and green eyes who stood in a small cluster of people about twenty feet from the sidewalk. "I recognize her from the picture by her column in *Teen Scene*."

At that moment Kelly turned and caught sight of Bess and Nancy. She waved and started walking toward them, a big smile on her face. She wore a smart black jacket with brass buttons and epaulets, skinny black pants, and ankle-high black boots. "You've got to be Bess," she said when she reached them. "I recognize you from your photo. Hi!"

"Hi," said Bess, staring at the columnist. "I can't believe I'm actually meeting you. I mean, I read your column every week. It's the best."

"Can I quote you? I'm Kelly Conroy," the columnist said, and she extended her hand to Nancy. "You're not one of the contestants, are you? Bess makes eight—"

"No," answered Nancy quickly. "I'm just here with Bess. My name's Nancy."

"Excuse me, Kelly," said a tall, handsome man of about thirty who had joined them. "Bettina wants to talk to you about the group shot."

"Thanks, Thom." Kelly turned back to Bess and Nancy. "Well, I'll see you later, girls. Meanwhile, meet Thom Fortner. He's the public relations person for Smash Clothing and also for the contest. Thom, this is Bess Marvin, one of our finalists, and her friend Nancy."

"Oh, hello, Mr. Fortner," Bess gushed. "I just love Smash Clothes. I wear them all the time."

"That's nice to hear," Mr. Fortner told her. "And please, call me Thom."

"Thom! Thom!" Nancy turned and saw a tall

7

woman with frosted hair and dangling royal-blue earrings wave at him. "What are you doing? I need you here, too!"

"Sorry, Bettina. I didn't realize." The public relations man raised his eyebrows in an amused gesture. "Excuse me, ladies. When Bettina calls, we all answer."

"Bettina Vasquez works for Elan Agency," Bess told Nancy. "She runs the place for Monique Durand. That's what they told me when I called to make arrangements for my trip."

"Young lady!" Bettina was shouting over Kelly Conroy's head. "If you want to be in the shot, you'd better join us, too."

"Who, me?" Bess looked confused.

"Yes, darling, you," the woman said icily.

"She doesn't seem very nice. But then, a big shoot like this must mean a lot of pressure for her," Nancy said as they walked toward the others.

The closer they got, the more Bess seemed to freeze up. Nancy thought she knew why. Standing near the iron railing, with only Lake Michigan behind them, were seven of the tallest, most beautiful girls she had ever seen.

"I suddenly feel short," Bess whispered.

"It's called 'petite,'" Nancy said, patting her friend on the arm.

"Hi, you must be Bess," said a honey blonde with a wide smile and warm brown eyes. "I'm Maggie Adams."

"Hi," said Bess, studying her with obvious dismay. Maggie was tall and willowy. Her skin was luminous, and her features were perfect.

"Don't worry," Maggie said reassuringly. "You haven't missed a thing. We've been here for an hour, but they haven't taken a single shot yet."

"This is so unprofessional," said one of the girls, an ash blonde with catlike golden eyes.

"Have you worked as a model?" Bess asked.

"Of course I have," the girl snapped.

"But I thought this contest was only for amateurs," Bess murmured.

"Er—I worked for charities," the girl responded with an insincere smile.

"I'm Bess Marvin. This is my friend, Nancy Drew."

The girl nodded and turned her back on them. "When are they going to start shooting?" she complained to no one in particular. "It's freezing out here."

"That's Heather Richards," Maggie told them in a whisper. "She's from New York."

Heather was right, though. The wind had begun to blow off the lake. Even for a fall day it was chilly. Nancy pulled up the collar of her light wool jacket and stuffed her hands into her pockets.

"Everybody," Maggie was saying, "this is Bess Marvin and her friend Nancy. Now let's see if I can remember all the names! Bess, you've already met Heather. This is Trudy Woo, Carey Harper, Alison Williams, Diana Amsterdam, and Natasha." One by one the lovely girls nodded and introduced themselves.

"Hi, Bess and Nancy," said Trudy Woo. She had glossy black hair, cut blunt and in bangs, and sparkling almond-shaped eyes.

Next to Trudy stood tall, slender Carey Harper. Her dark hair was twisted into a thick French braid, giving her a soft, classic look. "Welcome," Carey said, taking Bess in with a pair of amazing blue eyes that seemed to leap from her face when she smiled.

"Hi," Bess gulped before she turned to her next competitor.

"We wondered when you were going to get here," the girl said with a warm smile. "I'm Alison Williams." Alison was tall, like Maggie and Carey, but her skin was a rich chocolate brown, set off by large, glowing black eyes. Her glossy jet-black hair was parted on one side and held in place with a simple gold clip.

"Hi, Bess, I'm Diana," the next girl said. Diana's face had a delicate elfin quality, with mischievous aquamarine eyes. Diana and Trudy weren't quite so tall as the others. But Nancy noticed with dismay that Bess was by far the shortest of the contestants.

Natasha, who nodded at Bess and Nancy from the end of the group, had full, pouting lips, a short, slender nose, and enormous green eyes.

All in all, Nancy had to admit that the Face of the Year contestants were a pretty impressive-looking group. Bess shook hands with each girl in turn.

"I'm sorry," Bess said when she got to Natasha, "I didn't get your last name."

"It's just Natasha," the girl said with a thick European accent.

"That's beautiful," Bess said. "I'm never going to remember everyone's name, though."

"Don't worry," Maggie said. "There's no test. And besides, we have plenty of time to get to know one another. We'll be here all week."

"Okay! Okay, girls! Listen up!" Bettina Vasquez was clapping her hands and shouting to get everyone's attention. "We're ready for the first shot! Line up in this order, please! In the back row, Heather Richards, Natasha, Carey

Harper, and Alison Williams. Maggie Adams, Trudy Woo, Diana Amsterdam, and Bess Marvin, you'll be in front."

"Excuse me, Bettina, may I talk to you a moment?" Heather Richards said politely as the girls began taking their places.

"Could I please stay in the front?" Nancy heard Heather ask. "I'm terribly afraid of the water."

Bettina rolled her eyes impatiently and waved a hand. "Maggie Adams, you're tall. Would you please change places with Heather?"

"Sure," soft-spoken Maggie answered.

None of the other girls said anything when Heather rejoined them, but Nancy could tell they found the blond New Yorker less than charming.

"Okay, ladies." A bearded photographer wearing a red sweatshirt and gray jeans stepped out in front of the group. "I want you each to make sure you can see the lens. Some of you in front may have to scrunch down a little—"

"Wait for me," a man's voice rang out. Nancy turned around. A tall, incredibly handsome blond man with chiseled features was rushing up to the girls. Nancy recognized him from dozens of commercials, although she didn't know his name. "I'm in this shot, too!"

"Roger Harlan!" Bess shrieked, totally forgetting her cool.

"That's my name," he said with a dazzling smile that reached all the way up to his perfect blue eyes. "Sorry I'm late. I was filming a commercial."

"Roger, move in between Alison and Maggie, would you, darling?" Bettina asked. She and the handsome model obviously knew each other.

"Okay, folks," the photographer explained. "Pretend the lens is your best friend. You're just standing—"

The photographer's words were interrupted by a sharp crack. The contestants were all screaming as the iron railing behind them gave way. Before Nancy—or anyone—could react, there was a splash—one of the girls had plunged headlong into the lake!

Chapter

Two

Nᴀɴᴄʏ ᴅᴀsʜᴇᴅ to the edge of the pier, ready to dive in. But Roger Harlan had beat her to it. His shoes were off, and he was in the water in an instant.

Maggie Adams's head broke the surface. "Help! P-please!" she sputtered desperately. "I-I'm not a good swimmer." She spit out a mouthful of water.

Everybody crowded around, staring silently at the two figures in the water. "The rail must have rusted," Thom Fortner said to Bettina. "Stay calm," Roger was saying to Maggie as he threw an arm across her chest. "I'll get you out." He swam with her to the edge of the pier, where Thom reached down to pull her to safety. Panting for breath, Roger boosted himself onto the pier as everyone applauded.

Shivering, Maggie tried to reassure the people on the pier. "I'm f-fine," she faltered. "Thanks to Roger. I'm just cold, and my heart is pounding like crazy."

Shrugging out of her wool jacket, Nancy draped it around Maggie's shoulders. Maggie flashed her a grateful look.

Flash! Flash! A reporter from one of the daily Chicago papers was snapping pictures of the drenched girl. Her soaked hair hung in stringy ropes over her face, and she was missing both shoes. With her shoulders hunched against the chill wind, Maggie appeared to be small and scared.

"Nice human-interest filler," he said to one of the crew members. "I love when they fall in your lap."

"Please don't take any more pictures," Thom pleaded.

"Sorry, buddy," the reporter said with a shrug. "It's a free country, remember? The people have a right to know. Hey, Roger, that's great.

Keep your arms around her! Boy, the readers are gonna eat this up—'Prince Charming Saves Drowning Beauty! Could this mean romance?'"

"How rude," Kelly Conroy said as the reporter walked away laughing. "Are you okay, Maggie?"

Maggie smiled bravely through chattering teeth. "I—I think s-so." She looked up at Roger gratefully, and he smiled back down at her. Nancy wasn't the only one who noticed the attraction between them. She saw Heather Richards staring at the drenched couple. If Heather wasn't crazed with jealousy, she was doing a great imitation.

"This means I won't be in the shoot, doesn't it?" Maggie said, blinking away her tears.

"It's not really part of the contest," Kelly Conroy said, trying to comfort her. "It's just a publicity shot."

"I know," Maggie said weakly, "but my family will be disappointed." A big gust of wind blew off the lake, and Maggie shuddered.

"You're going to freeze out here!" Kelly said. "And the last thing you need is to catch a cold!"

"I'm pretty cold, too," Roger Harlan said, tightening his grip around Maggie's shoulders. "Why don't I take you back to your hotel, and we can both get dry and warm?" Maggie returned his intense look with a startled but pleased one of her own.

"Okay," she said, nodding.

She and Roger hurried to a cab someone had flagged down for them. Everyone watched them slip inside, two shivering figures now huddled together for warmth in the back seat. Nancy glanced over at Heather, who clenched her hands into fists so tightly that her knuckles were white.

"Well, the Face of the Year is off to quite a start," Kelly said to Nancy as they watched the shot being reset.

"I'm surprised the city doesn't check these railings more often," Nancy said, wondering if iron railings did just give way. "That was really dangerous. Maggie could have hit her head on one of those huge boulders lining the pier." Was it an accident, she wondered, or was it planned?

"I know," Kelly agreed. "It's scary."

"Help! I'm—*sputter, sputter*—not a good swimmer!" Nancy heard someone imitating Maggie's desperate cry. She turned in the direction of the voice.

While the crew repositioned the lights Heather

17

Richards had walked up to the photographer and was now doing a bad imitation of Maggie. "Imagine the picture that reporter got of her. She looked like a drowned rat. It should be charming," she purred.

The photographer was obviously uncomfortable, but Heather continued anyway. "Oh, and that hair! Don't you just love the dead mermaid look?"

Nancy walked over to where the other girls were standing.

"What a witch!" Bess seethed. "How can she be yukking it up at a time like this?"

"Oh, Heather thinks we're *all* a riot," Alison Williams remarked quietly. "When I told her I was from Tennessee, she asked me if it was really in the United States."

"And according to her, only blue-eyed people should use blue eyeliner," Trudy Woo added saucily. "She said it looks 'weird' on someone like me."

"Really? She told me my jacket would look great in a stable," Carey Harper joined in.

"She said my haircut was 'totally retro.' What was that supposed to mean?" Diana Amsterdam wondered aloud, fingering her mop of black curls.

"I don't think it was anything nice." Trudy

18

narrowed her eyes and glared at Heather, who was still flirting with the photographer.

"Well, she may not have been nice to any of us, but I notice she's been as sweet as pie to the people from Smash and Elan," Alison said.

Nancy stepped away from the contestants and wandered closer to Heather.

"Can you imagine?" Heather was telling the photographer. "I was supposed to be standing in Maggie's spot. That could have been me!"

Yes, thought Nancy, nodding her head slowly. It could have been. . . .

She looked more closely at the iron railing next to her. It had a simple design composed of vertical bars that gleamed in the afternoon sun. If Nancy guessed right, the railing wasn't more than a few years old.

"People! Can we *finally* get started?" Bettina wailed. "Remember, Elan is *paying* for this shoot!"

"Let's do it." The photographer stepped in front of the girls. "Let's get a few with your arms out wide. Careful of the people next to you. And now, big smiles!" the photographer told them.

Nancy looked over at the contestants and smiled. Bess was finally getting her first taste of modeling.

Taking a deep breath, Nancy strolled casually

back to where they'd first been shooting. She moved right up to the broken railing.

With a gasp, she reached out to touch it. Thom Fortner had been wrong. The railing wasn't rusty at all. In fact, it was almost perfectly smooth—except for the jagged markings of a saw.

It seemed that someone had cut through that railing on purpose!

Chapter

Three

STARTLED, NANCY STARED at the broken railing and then glanced down at the pier. Tiny metal shavings were gleaming in the fading sun. There was no doubt about it—the railing *had* been sawed.

As she fingered the edge of the broken railing once more, the word *sabotage* came to mind. But *why?* Why would anyone want to sabotage a modeling contest? Come on, Nancy, she told herself. It's probably just a simple case of vandalism.

Walking back toward the contestants, Nancy looked for Thom Fortner. As public relations director of the Face of the Year contest, Thom ought to know what was going on, Nancy thought.

He was sitting on a bench, a black leather briefcase open on his lap. When Nancy approached he shut the case and smiled at her.

"Hi," he said, his brown eyes lively. "Can I help you with something?"

"There's something I think you should see," Nancy said.

"Is it terribly important?" Thom asked, a small line creasing his forehead. "We're already behind schedule, and—"

"It's about the broken railing," Nancy told him. "I think you should see it."

Thom stood up, sighing heavily. Despite his obvious reluctance, he followed Nancy.

"You thought the fence must have been rusty, but it isn't. And look at these tiny jagged saw marks, and that pile of metal shavings. This railing was sawed through!"

Thom seemed taken aback. He examined the shavings for a moment, then got up and shrugged. "Well, I can't pretend to understand why vandals do what they do. Thanks for pointing it out, Nancy." Flashing her a smile, he began walking away.

"Wait!" Nancy called, trotting up beside him. "That was a serious accident! Maggie could have been badly hurt."

"Yes," Thom replied, walking back to his bench. "She was lucky. We all were."

"And what if it wasn't the work of vandals?" Nancy pressed.

Thom stopped in his tracks and gave Nancy a startled look. "What's that supposed to mean?"

"Suppose someone was out to get Maggie, or one of the other girls. Shouldn't you call the police?"

Thom seemed amused. "Young lady, I must say, you have quite an imagination—an *overactive* imagination."

"So you're not going to tell anyone?" Nancy asked.

"Of course I am. I'll be sure to contact the city to let them know the railing needs to be repaired," Thom said, sitting down. "And I'm sure when they see it they'll think exactly what I think—that vandals cut the railing."

Thom didn't want to talk about it anymore, which he made clear with a pleasant but dismissive smile. "Now I have to get back to some really important work, Nancy," he said apologetically. "Would you like a quick peek at the pairings for tomorrow night's banquet? We're bringing in some of Elan's top male models to escort the girls."

"I'd love to see the list," Nancy said, willing to play it light. Maybe Thom Fortner was right. Maybe the cut railing was the work of vandals. Chicago was a big city, with big-city problems.

"Can you keep a secret?" Thom winked at her.

"Usually," she said, disarmed.

Thom fished through his papers and pulled one out. "Here it is. Top secret stuff," he said, winking again. "I think Maggie Adams will be happy when she sees this."

Maggie Adams had been paired with Roger Harlan. Bess had drawn a fellow named Ernest Mullins. Though Nancy had never heard of him, Bess probably had. She studied fashion magazines and knew every model in the business.

They were interrupted then by the sound of one person clapping. Nancy saw the photographer giving the contestants a hand. "That's it, girls. We're done," he said as the crew started dismantling the lights. "You were great."

Bettina Vasquez nodded her approval. "Very nice, girls. If you'll give me your attention," she said loudly, "we're finished for now, so you can get back to the hotel. Tonight, at dinner you'll be meeting"—Bettina paused dramatically—"Monique Durand."

A ripple of excited murmurs broke the silence. Even Nancy knew that Monique Durand was the head of Elan Modeling Agency. A nod from her could send a girl to the heights of a dazzling modeling career.

"I also want to mention the banquet tomorrow night. You'll be wearing designer dresses, so you've got to find a few minutes tomorrow morning for a fitting. Please don't tell anyone what your dress is like, though. The designs are top secret until the banquet. Each of you will be paired with a top Elan male model for the evening. His name will be given to you tonight."

Another excited murmur passed through the group. Nancy noticed Bess's eyes light up.

"But I'm sorry to say," Bettina went on in an amused but dry voice, "only one of you will be lucky enough to get Roger Harlan for an escort. And if you *don't* get Roger, don't blame me. Thom Fortner is making up the pairs. Those are the breaks, girls. Modeling can be a tough business."

Soft laughter went through the group. But

Nancy noticed Heather Richards wasn't laughing. She was staring at Thom Fortner. Nancy wondered what Heather's reaction would be when she found out Maggie Adams was to be Roger's date.

While they waited for the bus to take them back to the hotel, Nancy spoke with the lighting crew.

"Get the four hundred twenty's in the truck first, Pat," a middle-aged man was saying to a young man in a plaid shirt. "And have the gaffers roll up the cable."

When the middle-aged man saw Nancy, he greeted her pleasantly. "How come you're not in the contest?" he asked with a smile. "You're as pretty as any of the other girls."

"Oh, thank you," Nancy told him, feeling herself blush a little. "I don't want to interrupt you," she continued, "but I noticed that the place where the railing broke was sawed through."

Both men's eyes widened. "You're kidding," the young man called Pat murmured. "Why would anyone pull a nasty stunt like that?"

"I don't know," Nancy answered. "But I'd like to find out." She led them over to the railing and showed them the saw marks. "Do you know what kind of saw could go through that?" she asked.

"I suppose you could get through it with a

hacksaw," the older man said slowly. "I have one in the truck. Want to see it?"

"Sure," Nancy told him. The middle-aged man led Nancy back to the truck.

"Come to think of it," he offered, "we had the truck parked right in front of that spot when we did our setup this morning. The truck could have hidden anybody cutting the railing."

"Who was here then?" Nancy asked, staring up into his blue-green eyes.

The lighting man shrugged his shoulders and laughed. "Honey, this is a public pier. Anybody could've been here."

He leapt onto the back of the truck and held out a hand for Nancy. She was struck by how immense the truck was.

"Now, a hacksaw is a pretty small tool," the lighting man explained, kneeling down beside a large red toolbox. "Let's see . . ." He opened the box and began rummaging around in it.

Nancy knelt beside him, leaning over to peer inside.

"Here it is," the man said, holding up a small saw with a pistol-grip handle.

But Nancy wasn't looking at the saw. Instead her eyes were riveted on the bottom of the toolbox. Reaching in, she picked up a tie tack. Gold initials were set in an onyx base.

The initials were RH.

"Is this yours?" she asked the man.

He studied the tie tack carefully. "Nope. I don't even wear ties. Besides, my initials are CM. None of my guys have those initials—"

But Nancy knew someone who did—Roger Harlan!

Chapter

Four

ROGER HARLAN. Could he have sawed through the railing? Why would he do it? Nancy wondered.

Roger claimed he'd been filming a commercial all day. But had he? They had only his word for it.

Before Nancy continued to speculate about Roger Harlan she realized she had to make sure the tie tack was really his.

"If you don't mind, I'll take this with me," she said to the lighting man. "I think I know whose it is, and I can return it." What I'd really like to know is how it got here, she added silently.

"I'm so hungry I could just *die.*" Bess looked as if she meant every word. Every time one of the white-jacketed waiters passed through the small banquet room reserved for Face of the Year participants, she practically fainted.

"Me, too," Nancy agreed. It had been a long day, and they realized they'd forgotten to eat lunch. Breakfast had been hours before. No wonder they were famished. "But help is on the way. Here comes a waiter with menus for us."

As the waiter handed the two girls large engraved menus, Nancy considered telling Bess what she'd discovered that day. But the last thing she wanted to do was ruin Bess's good time.

"Look, Nan," Bess said excitedly. "They have shrimp scampi!"

"One of your favorites," said Nancy. "Well, that makes things easy. I'll have the filet of sole." Closing her menu, Nancy sat back and smiled at her friend.

Bess was frowning. "I can't get scampi, Nancy," she said. "It's cooked in butter. Do you know how many calories are in one tiny little pat of butter? Billions!"

The waiter had walked up to the table, his

pencil poised to take their order. "Are you ready?"

Nancy ordered her sole. Then Bess asked for a green garden salad and whole-wheat toast, no butter.

Nancy rolled her eyes to the gilt-painted ceiling. "Bess, just because you don't want to gain weight doesn't mean you have to starve yourself! We missed lunch, remember?"

"Nancy Drew, you were born thin," Bess said, sounding a little irritated. "Don't tell me how to order, okay?"

"Sorry," Nancy apologized. It wasn't like Bess to snap at her. Nancy understood—Bess was under a lot of pressure.

Glancing around the dining room, Nancy saw that most of the other models had ordered very light meals, too. Alison Williams, sitting with a woman who had to be her mother, was munching on hearts of celery, and Carey Harper had barely touched her London broil before she asked the waiter to take it away.

"Look! There's Roger Harlan," Bess whispered excitedly, pointing to the door.

Nancy turned to watch Roger step into the room. Thom Fortner was with him, and the two men seemed to be chatting amicably.

"Isn't he adorable?" Bess murmured.

31

Nancy watched as Roger and Thom separated. Roger walked over to where Bettina was sitting, and Thom seemed to be heading for Kelly Conroy's table.

Before he could get there, Heather Richards took Thom by the arm and led him off to the side of the room.

That's strange, Nancy thought as she watched Heather buttonhole Thom. Whatever she was telling him made him appear glum. Heather, on the other hand, seemed animated and happy about the conversation.

"It's worth it. It's all worth it. No pain, no gain," Bess chanted as she looked down at the meager dinner the waiter had set before her. She picked up her fork and stabbed her salad, but all the time her eyes were hungrily attacking Nancy's appetizer.

"Have a stuffed mushroom, Bess," Nancy offered.

"Oh, all right, you convinced me." Instantly Bess's fork was on Nancy's plate. "Super," she pronounced, her mouth full of the succulent mushroom. "Can I have another?"

"Of course," Nancy said, pushing the plate closer to Bess.

Thom and Heather were walking to their tables now. Heather returned to hers while Thom went to the table occupied by Kelly Conroy and a regal-looking chestnut-haired woman in a white woolen suit. Although Fortner said hello and smiled at everyone as he passed by, Nancy noticed that his smile didn't reach his eyes.

"That older woman in white, sitting with Thom and Kelly," Bess said excitedly, "is Monique Durand. Isn't she gorgeous?"

Nancy moved her head to get a better look at the world-famous former model Monique Durand. When Nancy and Bess were young children, her perfect face had been plastered everywhere. Now she was the creator and owner of Elan Modeling Agency. Though she had to be thirty-five, Monique was as lovely as ever.

"Achoo!" A sudden burst from the table directly behind theirs made Nancy's head snap.

"Oh, sorry." Maggie Adams apologized to the room in general for her ear-splitting sneeze. Aside from her single sneeze, Maggie seemed fully recovered from her spill into the lake. She was radiant in a pale blue angora sweater.

Trudy Woo, who was sitting with Maggie, had burst out laughing at Maggie's sneeze. "I never heard anything like that!" Trudy said, still giggling.

"Isn't it awful?" Maggie included Nancy and Bess as well as Trudy in her conversation. "I've

33

always had this incredibly loud sneeze. No matter how hard I try to make it quieter, it always comes out like that!"

The clinking of a spoon against a glass brought everyone's attention to the table where Monique Durand had risen to her feet.

"Hello, everyone," Monique said in an accent that was faintly French and thoroughly charming. "I am Monique Durand. I want to thank you all for participating in our Face of the Year contest. We had more entrants this year than ever before, so you are very special young ladies to have made it this far."

Nancy glanced across the table at Bess, who was beaming, drinking in every one of Monique Durand's words.

"When I was a young model new to this country," Monique was saying, "the biggest problem I had was meeting photographers and getting my first portfolio. I had to knock on many doors until someone gave me a chance. But I'm happy to announce that for you, assembling a portfolio will be much easier. Tonight each of you will be assigned a photographer who will create a portfolio for you, courtesy of Elan."

Monique let the girls react to this wonderful news with a small burst of applause before she began speaking again. "Tomorrow your first 'pro-

fessional assignment,' so to speak, will be a
sportswear spread. Later in the week you'll be
posing in formal wear, casual wear, and
sundresses. The clothing has all been supplied by
Smash! Unlike a real modeling assignment,
you're free to keep any clothes you wear."

"Wow! I didn't know we'd get to keep anything!" Bess said excitedly.

Monique continued, "We've been having un-
seasonably cool weather, and I'm sorry that
we've scheduled the sessions to be shot outdoors.
But modeling is hard work, girls. You might as
well learn that now. To be a successful model you
have to be willing to wear a sundress in cold
weather and a heavy coat in the summer. And
through it all you must smile, smile, smile. Our
profession requires a great deal of discipline. In
fact, lack of discipline is the reason most girls fail
to achieve the success they deserve."

Was Nancy imagining it, or had Monique
Durand aimed her remarks about discipline
straight at Bettina Vasquez? Bettina was glaring
at Monique. Except for Nancy, nobody seemed
to notice. Everyone else was totally captivated by
Monique.

"Also, remember—news reporters have been
invited to all the shoots this week," Monique
went on. "Since you will be representing the

sponsors of this contest, we expect you to be polite to them, no matter how nosy or rude they act. Above all, please don't do anything drastic with your appearance after your makeovers tomorrow morning. We'd like you stick with those results. Last year we had a contestant who streaked her hair during the third day of the contest. Streaked or frosted hair is out of date, and it reflects badly on all of us. And please, keep your makeup to a minimum. When in doubt, use less, not more."

There was no doubt about Monique's comment that time. Her crack about frosted hair was directed at Bettina. Nancy, and everyone else now, watched as the two women glared at each other with undisguised dislike. There was a moment of awkward silence.

"Achoo!" Maggie let out another megasneeze, which broke the tension in the room. Everyone chuckled, then applauded lightly for Monique as she sat down.

Thom Fortner rose to speak. He glanced around at the contestants with a gleam in his eye as he dug in his pocket for a piece of paper. "Well, I guess this is the moment you've all been waiting for," he said, joking. "I have the names of your escorts for tomorrow's banquet!"

Bess reached across the table and squeezed

Nancy's hand. "Maybe I'll get Roger Harlan!" she whispered. "Oh, I hope, I hope, I hope!"

"Maybe." Without giving the secret away, Nancy squeezed Bess's hand and grinned. "But I'm sure none of the escorts will be losers." She glanced over at Maggie Adams's table. She wanted to see the expression on the girl's face when she got the good news.

"Let me dispense with the mystery right away," a flushed Thom Fortner said. He cleared his throat. "Excuse me. Heather Richards, your date for the banquet will be—Roger Harlan!"

Chapter
Five

NANCY'S MOUTH FELL OPEN. As the other girls whispered among themselves, Heather beamed, casting a smug glance at the disappointed Maggie. Nancy tried to catch Thom Fortner's eye, but he studiously avoided her gaze. No wonder!

Maggie Adams had been chosen to be Roger's escort, but at the last moment, Thom changed her assignment. Why?

Thom took a pen from his breast pocket and made a quick correction on the sheet of paper he was holding. "Moving right along," he said after the pause, "Alison Williams, your escort will be Daryl Hancock. Bess Marvin, you'll be paired with Ernest Mullins. Carey Harper, your date is Jason Tyler. . . ."

Thom went on giving out the assignments, and Nancy peered around the room. Heather Richards was wearing a huge, triumphant smile as she waved to Roger Harlan. Roger was seated next to Bettina and didn't seem to notice Heather at all.

Nancy reached into the pocket of her slacks and fingered the gold tie tack with the initials RH on it. How had it gotten into the toolbox? She decided she had to ask Roger.

"Ernest Mullins is one of the best-looking men in the entire galaxy," Bess was saying. "He's got the most incredible dimple in his chin. He works *all* the time. He's in practically every magazine there is."

"That's great, Bess," Nancy said.

"Are you having a good time?" Kelly Conroy's bubbly voice came out in a whisper, since Thom was still giving out assignments. The *Teen Scene* reporter had a pencil and pad in her hand as she leaned over Bess and Nancy's table. "Bess," she began, "I'd like to set up a time to interview you."

39

"You want to interview *me* for *Teen Scene?*" Bess gasped.

"Sure," Kelly said with a smile. "We're doing a few paragraphs on each of the contestants. It'll be one of the feature articles in the next issue."

"But I've never been interviewed before in my entire life! How will I know what to say?" Bess was babbling and obviously more than a little nervous.

"Oh, it's easy," Kelly said with a smile. "I'll just ask about you, your friends, your hobbies, what you like to do, stuff like that. How's tomorrow after your makeover?"

"Sure, that'll be fine," said Bess, thrilled and scared at the same time.

"Now, on to photographers," Thom said as he riffled through his jacket pocket for another sheet of paper. "Let's see—Diana Amsterdam, your portfolio photographer will be John Colao. Carey Harper, you've been assigned Terry Porter. Bess Marvin, you'll be photographed by Alex Bogorofsky—"

"Alex Bogorofsky!" Bess managed to keep her voice down, but her enthusiasm was tuned way up high. "He only takes movie stars' photos!"

"You can't do better than Bogorofsky. He's world class," Kelly said. "Congratulations, Bess."

"Oh, this is so, so, so, so exciting," Bess said with a sigh. "I just hope my makeover turns out all right."

"You'll be in good hands, Bess," Nancy said. "I don't think you should worry about it."

"They've never had a failure at Mr. La Fortune's yet," Kelly added.

The photographers had all been assigned, and now Monique Durand was standing to give her final remarks. "It's past nine," she said, glancing at the diamond watch on her wrist. "To bed, everyone! A good night's rest is essential for success in modeling. We'll see you early tomorrow."

"Good night, Kelly. Come on, Nan! I've got to get to sleep immediately!" Bess said, rising from the table and getting her handbag. "Yesterday I noticed I was starting to get circles under my eyes."

"Bess," Nancy groaned, waving good night to Kelly and following her friend, "you do *not* have circles under your eyes."

"Can you imagine, Nancy? Alex Bogorofsky? Taking *my* picture?" Bess seemed to float out of the dining room to the elevator. "It's going to be so much fun being famous!"

Nancy pressed the button for the elevator as Natasha and an older woman who looked like her mother walked up speaking in a foreign language.

"Hello. Who is your photographer again?" Natasha asked Bess.

Nancy knew that Bess was trying to downplay her feelings when she answered. "Oh, Alex Bogorofsky."

Natasha's green eyes widened. When they stepped into the elevator, she admitted her feelings in an outright and charming manner. "I am so jealous!"

Bess smiled and shrugged. "I can bet. I'm even jealous of myself!"

That made them all laugh.

"Good night," Bess called out as she and Nancy reached their floor. "Oh, Nancy. Isn't life beautiful?"

"It certainly is," Nancy replied, getting the key out of her bag. She opened the door for Bess, who floated into the room and flopped down on her bed.

"The Bogorofsky Portraits," Bess said with a sigh. "That's what they call his annual show at the Hollywood Palace. Maybe I'll be in it next year!"

"But, Bess, isn't that for established stars?" Nancy asked gingerly.

"By this time next year I could *be* an established star, Nancy."

There was no sense arguing, Nancy thought as she began changing into a nightgown. She was terribly concerned for her friend. Bess's expectations of winning the contest and going on to instant stardom could leave her very hurt.

"I'm going to wash up, Bess." Nancy walked into the bathroom and took a thick white washcloth off the towel rack.

"Wait, Nancy! Look!" Bess called frantically from the other room.

Nancy hurried back and saw Bess leaning into the mirror over her bureau. She was wearing a look of horrified alarm. "I can't believe this!" she moaned, pointing to a tiny red blotch on her cheek. "This is terrible! I'm getting a pimple— an enormous, gigantic, humongous one!"

"Calm down, Bess," Nancy said, deftly swiping at the red mark with her washcloth. "That enormous, gigantic, humongous pimple is just a little ol' piece of tomato."

"Morning, Nancy!" Bess called out brightly as a beam of sunlight landed on Nancy's pillow.

"Morning." Nancy wiped the sleep from her eyes and yawned. "What time is it?"

"Almost seven-thirty," Bess said, all dressed and ready for the day. She pulled a small piece of paper from the top of her dresser. "This was slid under our door last night. It's my agenda. What a day! First my makeover, then the interview, a dress fitting, the sportswear shoot, and tonight the banquet! So, Nan," Bess added, floating back to earth, "what do *you* have on for today?"

Tracking down Roger Harlan, Nancy thought. She hoped to find out whether the model was implicated in the railing sabotage.

"Earth to Nancy!" Bess said with a wry grin. "I asked you what you're doing today."

"Oh," Nancy fibbed, not wanting to bring up anything even potentially upsetting, "I guess I'll go to the Art Institute."

"Morning, Bess and Nancy!" a girl called from the hall.

"That must be Maggie," Bess explained. "Last night I told her to knock on our door when she was ready to go to breakfast."

"You go. I'll meet you downstairs," Nancy said, not wanting to hold up Bess and Maggie.

"Okay—if you're sure." Bess waltzed out the door without waiting for an answer. "Morning, Maggie," Nancy heard her say. "Isn't life beautiful?"

Nancy made it downstairs as Bess and the

other contestants were leaving for their make-overs.

"Take a good look, Nan!" Bess called out from the dining room door. "You may never see me looking like this again!"

"Good luck!" Nancy waved a last goodbye to Bess and the others and touched the tie tack in her pocket. Then she turned to Kelly Conroy, who was also leaving the dining room. "Kelly, where are Elan's offices?" she asked.

Since Roger was a signed client at Elan, Nancy thought they'd know where he'd be that day.

"They're on Illinois Avenue," Kelly told her as they stepped out of the dining room. "Are you going over there now?"

"I thought I might," Nancy said, hoping that Kelly wouldn't ask her why.

"Well, maybe I'll see you there," Kelly told her with a breezy smile. "I have to drop some copy off later. Monique gets to approve every word I write about her agency."

Just as they approached the revolving door Kelly stopped suddenly. "Yikes! I left my work in the dining room. Wait while I get it, okay?"

"Sure," Nancy said.

The lobby of the Inter-Continental Hotel was sleek and luxurious. Nancy was admiring the black lacquered tables and deep red plush couches when she heard someone moan, "How could I be so dumb?"

Nancy turned and saw two bellhops talking to each other not far from where she stood. One was a short, red-haired man, and the other was a tall, thin, balding man.

"Mr. Johnson is going to blow his stack," the balding one said.

"I know," the redhead agreed. "When he gave me that passkey he said, 'Guard it with your life'!"

"And you're sure it didn't slip off the key ring somewhere?"

The redhead shrugged helplessly. "I had it yesterday, when all those models and the people from the clothing company checked in. But this morning when I went to find it, it was gone."

Suddenly the balding man seemed to notice Nancy. He poked his colleague in the ribs, and the two fell silent. Not surprising, thought Nancy —no hotel employee is going to advertise the fact that a passkey is missing.

"Here I am!" Kelly came trotting toward Nancy. She was waving a fat manila envelope in one hand.

"Thanks for waiting," Kelly said with a smile.

Nancy flicked her eyes over Kelly as the two

girls pushed through the exit and stepped out onto the avenue. Kelly might be a good source of information—about Roger Harlan, about Thom Fortner, even about Monique and Bettina. A columnist for *Teen Scene* magazine was bound to know most of the gossip.

"Taxi?" the doorman asked the two girls.

"Not for me, thanks," Kelly said, turning to Nancy. "I've got to run this by my office before I go up to Elan. Maybe I'll see you there." With that, she hurried off into the sunny, cold day.

"I'll take a cab," Nancy told the doorman, who put up a gloved hand for her right away.

Nancy rode up to the twenty-fifth floor of the Century Building and into a world of white. White marble flooring, white lacquered furniture, and white-on-white wallpaper printed with the Elan logo adorned the office. Brass poster-size frames lined the walls. In them were featured some of the world's most beautiful women and men. Several were of Monique Durand and her top models on a Caribbean sailing excursion.

"May I help you?" a sultry young receptionist asked Nancy.

"Can you tell me where I can find Roger Harlan?" Nancy asked.

"I expect him in later this morning. Do you have an appointment to see him?" the receptionist asked.

"No, I don't," Nancy said apologetically. "But I found something valuable that I think is his. I'd like to give it to him."

"Well, have a seat," the receptionist told her, motioning to the white leather couches that surrounded a low, square table piled with fashion magazines.

"Thanks." Nancy sat down and picked up a glossy magazine. One of its pages was dog-eared. Curious, Nancy flipped to the marked page. Inside was an interview with a woman named Trina Evans. Nancy scanned the article and learned that Trina Evans was the creator and owner of Let's Go, Smash's major competitor in the clothing business.

Shown in the accompanying picture, Trina was a willowy blonde with green eyes and bangs cut straight across her salon-tanned forehead. She wore a stunning Egyptian-looking bronze necklace. Someone had circled one of her comments in pencil. "Promotional contests like Face of the Year are shallow attempts to capture the public's attention. They represent the lowest level of marketing, in my opinion. Let's Go will never involve itself with such nonsense."

When the people from Elan or Smash had read this article, it must have made them see red, Nancy thought with an amused grin.

Nancy tossed the magazine back onto the low table. She was restless. Fashion magazines weren't on her mind.

If Roger Harlan had stolen the saw and sabotaged the railing, why did he jump into the lake to save Maggie? To divert suspicion from himself, Nancy reasoned. But why would Roger Harlan want to sabotage the Face of the Year contest in the first place?

Nancy's hands were smudged from handling the magazine. "Where's the ladies' room, please?" she asked the receptionist.

"Right down the hall," the woman answered, pointing into the inner offices of the agency. "Second left after Bettina Vasquez's office."

"Thanks," Nancy said, pushing through the glass door and starting down the corridor.

"Hello, dear," she heard a voice call when she passed an office. Nancy stopped. Inside, Bettina Vasquez was standing behind a white-lacquered desk. "You're Bess Marvin's friend. Right?"

"Right," Nancy answered. "Hi."

"Are you interested in modeling?" Bettina asked, peering at Nancy over a pair of oversize flamingo-pink glasses. "Your friend Bess is a little on the short side, but *you* might really be able to have a career, if you want."

Nancy felt bad when Bettina mentioned Bess's height. Bettina was confirming Bess's worst fears about her size.

"Don't be shy," Bettina added. "Come in. I have a minute or two."

Nancy stepped into the modeling executive's office. Bettina's carpet was a deep royal blue, and a blue-and-white loveseat stood out against the white walls. Photos in hot pink frames of a younger Bettina were arranged in clusters on the walls.

"I'm really not interested in modeling as a career," Nancy admitted, smiling at Bettina, who was staring hard at her.

"Well, if you change your mind, let me know," Bettina said with a smile. "With your red hair and blue eyes, you'd be a big hit."

"Sorry," Nancy said. "But modeling's just not for me."

Bettina seemed almost lonely, as if she needed to talk to someone. "Well, what brings you to Elan then?"

Unable to think of a good story, Nancy decided to come right out with the truth. "I found something that belongs to Roger Harlan," she said.

"Oh? Well, you can give it to me. I'll see that he gets it." Bettina held out her hand.

"Er, no," Nancy said, hedging. Giving her real reason for being there was one thing. Handing over her only piece of evidence was another. "I'd—uh—rather give it to him myself. I—well, he's so handsome." It was the first thing she could think to say.

It wound up being perfect. "Say no more," said Bettina, giving Nancy a little wink. "Oh, I'd better get to the hotel. Look at the time. Is it terribly chilly out?"

"It's brisk," Nancy answered.

"Oh, dear, that means it'll feel freezing to me," Bettina said. "I'd better take a coat."

Bettina opened her closet.

Nancy gasped out loud at what she saw hanging on the inside of the door. It was a poster-size portrait of Monique Durand—riddled with dozens of small red darts!

Chapter
Six

SLIPPING INTO HER COAT, Bettina giggled wick-
edly. "Are you shocked? Don't be," she said.
"Believe me, Monique is not the sweet person
she pretends to be. In fact, she deserves everything and anything she gets."

"Why?" Nancy asked. "What did she do?"

Bettina shook her head. "Oh, it's a long, sad
story. Let's just say that even though Monique
and I were once the best of friends, we're now the
best of enemies."

"If you feel like that, it must be hard to work with her," Nancy observed.

"Well, I won't be here much longer," Bettina replied. "When the contest is over I'm leaving Elan."

"To go where?"

Bettina raised her shoulders and shrugged. "Who knows? New York? Madrid? Paris? I only know I'm getting as far away from Chicago as I can. Will I see you at the hotel later?"

"I'll be there," Nancy replied as Bettina ushered her out of the office.

"See you later, then." Bettina gave her a brazen smile. "Don't think too badly of me, dear. If you knew the woman like I do, you'd want to take aim, too."

When Nancy got back to the reception area, she saw Kelly Conroy step off the elevator. Over her shoulder was a maroon handbag, and in her hand was a large manila envelope.

"Nancy, hi!" Kelly called out. She walked over to the receptionist's desk. "I'd like to leave this for Ms. Durand. Please tell her I need it back, with her comments, by tomorrow morning, okay?"

"Sure, Ms. Conroy," the receptionist answered. "By the way," she added, addressing

Nancy, "Roger Harlan called while you were in the ladies' room. He's doing a shaving cream commercial, and he'll be tied up all day."

"What are you doing now, Nancy?" Kelly asked, taking her in with a cool gaze.

Nancy smiled. "Got any exciting suggestions?"

"Well, I'm famished," Kelly said. "Want to go to lunch? I know a great little hole in the wall called Dominic's."

"Fantastic," Nancy agreed. She and Kelly rode down the elevator and walked a few blocks up a side street that branched off the avenue.

"Dominic's is kind of a journalists' hangout," Kelly told her as they walked. "It's dark and kind of seedy, but they have great potato skins. And here we are!" She pointed to a heavy wooden door.

"There's no sign," Nancy said. "How do people find this place?"

"Most people never do. That's what's neat about it." Kelly pushed through the door, and Nancy followed. The restaurant was furnished in dark colors. Kelly waved and smiled at the hostess, who gave them menus and led them to a bloodred leather booth in the back.

Kelly gazed at Nancy for a moment after they sat. Then she narrowed her green eyes and leaned forward. "Okay, let's level," she said. "What are you really doing at the Face of the Year contest?"

"I'm not sure what you mean," Nancy said, suddenly feeling uncomfortable.

Kelly raised her eyebrows. Then she reached for her big maroon handbag and began rummaging inside it. She pulled out a newspaper clipping and handed it across the table to Nancy. "I came across this when I was looking up Bess's hometown paper. That's you, isn't it?"

Nancy looked down at a picture of herself shaking hands with Chief McGinnis of the River Heights Police Department.

"You're Nancy Drew, the detective," Kelly said simply.

Nancy handed the newspaper clipping back to Kelly with a smile. "Yes, I'm Nancy Drew."

Kelly leaned in closer to Nancy. "I don't believe you're here just to have a good time with your friend. I think you're investigating something."

As Nancy scanned the menu, she wondered how frank she should be with Kelly.

"You can tell me the truth, Nancy," Kelly said after the waitress had taken their order.

"Only if you promise not to tell anyone what I say," Nancy said, bargaining.

"That's tough," Kelly said. "After all, I am a journalist—but okay."

Nancy told her everything that had happened so far. She finished by telling Kelly about the disquieting photo of Monique that Bettina had in her closet at work.

"Whew," said Kelly when Nancy was done. "Very interesting. You know, there's a lot of bad feeling in this contest."

"Oh?" Nancy's eyes widened. Kelly was confirming what Nancy had felt all along. "What kind of bad feeling?"

"Well, you've heard about Thom and Bettina, haven't you?" Nancy shook her head. "They were engaged. Until Thom got to know Monique, that is. Thom and Monique are dating now, from what I hear." Kelly paused long enough for the waitress to set their food down.

"No wonder Bettina hates Monique," Nancy murmured. "What about Roger Harlan? What do you know about him?"

Kelly shook her head helplessly. "Roger's a mysterious guy. I know he takes acting lessons and is pretty serious about his career. But it's kind of hard to get a handle on him. He told one of our photographers that he was unhappy at Elan. But the only way he can get out of his contract is if Elan fails to do a good job representing him."

"Well, if this contest gets botched, it won't look very good for Elan," Nancy said, reaching for her iced tea.

"Okay, Nancy. Where do we go from here?" Kelly propped her elbows on the table.

"How can we find out about Heather Richards?" Nancy asked. "Something is going on with her."

"I'll put some feelers out," Kelly promised. "We have pretty good connections at *Teen Scene.*"

"Great," said Nancy, giving Kelly a smile. She had a good feeling about the reporter, and it was fun to work with someone else. "Meanwhile, let's hope the contest goes smoothly from now on."

"Yikes!" said Kelly, glancing at her watch. "It's almost one-thirty. The girls are going to be at the park in an hour. I want to get their reactions to their makeovers and interview Bess!"

Nancy and Kelly ate quickly, hurried out of the restaurant, and hailed a cab. Soon they were at the Inter-Continental.

"I hope I haven't missed them!" Kelly cried.

But as she and Kelly stepped off the elevator,

they saw Bess standing with Carey Harper outside Alison Williams's door.

"How do you like my hair, Nan?" Bess said, shaking it out a little.

Nancy was amazed at what a difference the hairstylist had made by not curling Beth's hair but leaving it tousled and straight. "I like it," she said slowly. "It's like a lion's mane—but sophisticated and sexy. Anyway, I do love it, and the eye makeup, too." A fine aqua line edged the bottom of Bess's eyes, making them seem larger and rounder. Her thick lashes were covered in a fine layer of teal blue.

"Didn't they do a good job on Carey, too?" Bess said. "Doesn't she look super?"

"Bess, stop!" Carey Harper said with a modest blush. But Nancy thought Bess was right. Carey's dark hair had been cut to shoulder length, and she'd been given bangs, which made her eyes stand out.

"Mr. La Fortune did great work on you two," Kelly said, referring to the stylist who was responsible for the girls' makeovers. "You must be really happy."

Carey grimaced. "We are, but not everyone is. Alison won't even show her face," she said, turning and knocking on the door. "Allie. Open up!"

"Come on," Bess added. "You can't stay in there forever!"

"Oh, yes, I can!" came a tearful lament from the other side of the door.

"What happened?" Nancy asked.

"We're not sure," Bess answered. "She came back from her makeover wearing a turban. Then she ran into her room and double-locked the door."

"I'm going home," Alison shrieked from the other side of the door.

Diana Amsterdam appeared from up the hall, tapping lightly on Alison's door. "Please, Allie," she begged. "You can't drop out now."

"I don't want to—I *have* to!" Alison moaned on the other side of the door.

"Sometimes we think a new haircut makes us look terrible even when it doesn't," Kelly threw in. "Besides, you can't just hide in there all day."

"Right," Carey added. "What about the banquet? Don't you want to go?"

"Sure, I want to go," Alison said bitterly. "But I'll never be able to. Not after this!"

"Oh, come on, Alison, stop being silly," said Bess, trying a new tack. "Whatever you think of your makeover, it can't be *that* bad!"

"Oh, it can't, huh?" Alison shouted, undoing the chain lock and flinging the door open. She stood in front of them wearing a bright orange turban that complemented her dark skin.

"Still think I'm being silly?" she chided, reaching for the turban and pulling it off.

All the girls gasped at what they saw. Giant sections of Alison's hair were missing altogether —and what was left was burned into charred clumps of frizz!

Chapter
Seven

Everyone stood in silence, staring at Alison's head in horror.

"Do you still think I'm being silly?" Her lip trembling, Alison confronted the cluster of girls who stood outside her door, gaping at her. "Well, do you?"

"No!" Bess gasped.

"What's the problem here?" Monique Durand's distinctive voice came up behind them.

"Alison's makeover," Bess managed to murmur. "Her hair—"

61

"Argh!" Monique let out a little scream when she saw Alison, who had tears spilling down her cheeks now. "You poor, poor girl!" Monique cried, lifting a clump of what remained on Alison's head. "Come inside the room. We must talk."

Gently shooing the others away, Monique put an arm around Alison's shoulder and guided her back into her room. "When I was a young model in Paris I had a similar experience," Nancy heard her telling Alison before she shut the door.

"The bus is downstairs waiting to take you to Anderson Park," one of Bettina's young assistants, a girl named Jackie, called up and down the hall. "Let's go, everybody!"

"Coming with us, Nan?" Bess asked, lightly touching her friend on the arm.

"I'll meet you there, Bess," Nancy said, walking to the elevator with her.

Heather Richards poked her head out her door just then. "Wait for me!" she called to the girls. Heather's lustrous ash-blond hair was fastened back on one side with a comb, giving her an ultrasophisticated look that really worked. Even though Heather hadn't needed a makeover, the one she had gotten really suited her.

"We'll hold the door for you," Carey Harper

told Heather. Nancy could tell that Carey was used to being nice.

"No problem with Heather's makeover, I notice," Kelly whispered to Nancy as the beautiful ash blonde sauntered past them into the elevator.

"I think I should have a little talk with a hairdresser," said Nancy as she stepped into the elevator.

"Good idea," Kelly said quietly.

Pierre La Fortune had a wild perm himself. His hair, though thinning on top, flowed out in small blond ringlets behind his ears.

"I was sick, absolutely sick when I saw what happened to that sweet, sweet girl," he was telling Nancy. It was half an hour later.

She'd gotten his address from Elan and gone to the salon where the girls had had their makeovers. "But I tell you, it wasn't my fault!"

"I don't know how many people are going to agree with you about that, Mr. La Fortune," Nancy said as gently as she could.

Flopping down in a pink vinyl revolving chair, the hairdresser let out a howl. "I know! My reputation will be ruined! I only pray that this doesn't get into the papers. But if it does, I'll show them the materials I used! I put the same chemicals on that girl's hair that I've been using for years!"

"Do you have the empty bottles?" Nancy asked.

Pierre got up from his chair and pointed to the side of the room, where several pink enamel hairwashing tubs stood. "If they haven't been thrown away, they should be right over there."

Shaking his head, Pierre walked with Nancy over to the wash tubs. "Did you see the other girls I did? They looked lovely! Heather, Carey, Natasha." He shuddered at the memory of Alison Williams. "These are the empty containers. You see, they are all exactly alike! Like all the other containers we use here at Mr. Pierre's."

Uncapping one of the pink plastic containers, Nancy took a whiff of finishing solution. The second container smelled the same. But the third was distinctly different.

"Ugh," she said, handing the container to Pierre. "Smell this!"

"I *thought* something was wrong with the container, so I double-checked the date on it. See? It's fresh." Pierre pointed to the top of the container. According to the date, the product could be used safely for several months.

Nancy sniffed the container again. Memories of her high school chem lab came to mind. "This isn't a hair-finishing solution—it's some sort of caustic chemical!"

The hairdresser's eyes bulged wide. "But who would put caustic chemicals in my supplies?"

Nancy gazed steadily at the hairdresser. "That's what I intend to find out. Who exactly was in the salon this morning?"

"Only myself, my assistant, and the people from Face of the Year," he told her. "They had exclusive use of my shop for the day."

"May I keep this container?" Nancy asked, holding up the bottle with the offending solution.

"Please," Mr. Pierre lamented. "Get it out of here! I never want to see it again!"

The shoot was in progress by the time Nancy arrived at the Anderson Park exercise trail. Nancy's cab pulled up at the first exercise station just as Trudy Woo was making a turn over the parallel bars. Trudy must have had many gymnastics classes, Nancy thought, approaching the group. The girl was able to flash an easy smile in the direction of the camera even as her body twisted upside down.

Off to the side the other contestants stood waiting their turns. Most of the other girls had slipped on coats over their leotards and leg warmers.

Anderson Park had one of the best outdoor exercise facilities Nancy had ever seen. The aim of the shoot was to show each girl on a different piece of equipment.

Since it had rained the night before, the ground beneath most of the equipment was muddy even though the track itself was dry.

"Now let's have Heather Richards on the rings," the photographer said.

"She's in the trailer. She's having trouble with a contact lens," Bettina told the photographer. "Use someone else."

"Any volunteers?" the photographer asked.

Bess was giggling as she raised her hand and waved it.

"Okay." He pointed at Bess. "You're on."

Bess stepped forward and walked toward the rings, but stopped short of them. "It's really muddy under there," she said, staring at the ground.

The lighting man was at her side in a flash. "I'll hoist you up so you don't get dirty."

He lifted her up with a grunt, and Bess grabbed the rings. "This is hard!" she announced.

"But it looks good," the photographer said, rushing around the other side of the bar to get a different angle. "Okay, let's have a smile."

Bess managed a smile, though Nancy could tell

she was struggling madly to stay on the rings.
Bess wasn't noted for her athletic abilities. Her
idea of a hard workout was to give herself a
manicure.

"Now let's see you pull yourself up! Bend your
elbows, and let's have another smile."

"I can't," Bess said, gritting her teeth. "I just
can't!"

The photographer's response was a smile.
'That's nice, very nice. I want some sweat shots,
too."

"Ugh," Bess said, still struggling. Her look of
struggle quickly changed to one of panic when
one of the rings suddenly snapped! Unable to
hold herself up with one hand, Bess plunged into
the mud—face first.

"Oh, no!" Nancy cried, rushing to her friend.
'Are you okay?"

"Am I okay? Do I look okay?" Huge globs of
thick brown mud streaked down Bess's face, and
her outfit was totally ruined.

"I meant, did you break any bones," Nancy
said pointedly.

"No," Bess moaned. "But my hair! My face!"

As Bess's fellow contestants comforted her,
Nancy searched the ground under the rings.
Sticking up out of the mud was a bolt—or rath-
er half a bolt. It had been cut almost all the

way through. When Bess hung on it her weight snapped it in two.

As soon as Bettina looked at Bess, she made a face. "Bad luck," she said, without a lot of mercy. "Sorry, darling. You're out of this shoot. You might as well get back to the hotel and shower."

"But, Bettina," Bess protested, "I could wash up somewhere—"

"Here, pig. Here, piggie, piggie," Heather muttered. When the other girls stared at her, she only shrugged. "Lighten up, guys! I was only making a little joke."

Nancy noticed that Bess's hands were clenched into tight fists. "Come on, Bess. You'll look fine by tonight for the banquet."

"Arrgh! I could spit!" Bess said as soon as the others were out of earshot.

"It could have been a lot worse, Bess," Nancy said, leading her friend out of the park to a cab stand. "At least you didn't break any bones."

"Oh, that's great," Bess said sarcastically.

Nancy was quiet during the ride home. Until Bess simmered down, she decided the best thing she could do was to remain neutral.

By the time they reached the hotel, Bess's mood did seem to have brightened a little. "Oh, well," she muttered, "they say mud is good for the skin."

Nancy smiled and put an arm on her friend's shoulder. "That's the spirit," she said as they made their way to the elevator.

"You know something, Nancy? I'd like to eat a pastry the size of the Wrigley Building. Maybe that would make me feel better," Bess muttered as they got off the elevator and walked past Heather Richards's room to their suite.

"You know, Nan, why doesn't Heather get dumped in the mud or anything?"

"She's just been lucky," said Nancy.

"Nothing terrible has happened to Carey Harper, Diana Amsterdam, Trudy Woo, or Natasha, either.

"Know what I think?" Bess said bitterly, standing at the door of their room while Nancy unlocked it. "I think Heather Richards is jinxing this contest!"

Nancy thought it was time to change the subject. "Isn't it great to have somebody else pick up?" she said when they stepped into their room.

"It sure is," Bess agreed. "Well, I'm heading straight for the shower."

"Okay," Nancy said, flopping down on the bed. Her mind was whirling from the events of the day. Staring up at the ceiling, she found herself wondering about Roger Harlan. If Roger was behind the cut railing, he must also be the culprit behind the other incidents—Alison's hair disaster, Bess's dive into mud—but how had he done it? As far as Nancy could tell, Roger had been nowhere near Pierre's salon or Anderson Park.

Bess was out of the shower and freshly dressed by five.

"I'm positively famished, and the banquet doesn't start for three hours," she said. "Want to come with me to the coffee shop? I've got to eat *something.*"

"Sure," Nancy said, stretching and getting up.

They left the room and went into the hall. "Watch out!" a voice called from behind a clothing rack moving up the hall.

"Nancy!" Bess said as the rack rolled by her. "I bet those are the dresses we're wearing tonight! Don't you wish you could get a peek at them?"

Pulling Nancy by the arm, Bess took off after the rolling rack. "Hi," she said to the curly-haired boy pushing it. "Are those dresses from Smash?"

"Eight Smash formals," he answered with a grin. "They go to Suite Four-hundred-forty-four."

"That's them!" Bess told Nancy as she hurried along after him. "Wait!" she called to the boy. "Would you mind if we took a look at them? We won't be long." The smile she gave the delivery boy was irresistible.

Nancy wasn't surprised when he stopped pushing the rack. "Sure," he said, dazzled by her. "I'm early anyway."

"That's so sweet of you," Bess purred. She walked over to the rack and inspected the dress on one of the hangers. "Here's mine!"

Bess lifted a filmy sky-blue dress off the rack and held it out for Nancy to see. Like the others, the dress was covered in plastic that was easy to see through. Bess's dress was absolutely gorgeous. The neckline was low and wide, the waist and hips fitted, and at the knee the skirt flared out in flouncy ruffles.

"I adore it!" Bess said, taking the dress off the hanger and pretending to waltz.

"Are you girls in the contest?" the delivery boy asked.

Bess nodded modestly. "I am," she said.

Nancy flipped over a small tag around one of the hangers and pulled out a soft peach creation. "This one is Maggie's," she said, admiring the lovely silk dress.

"Oh!" Bess cried. "It'll be fantastic on her."

Putting Maggie's formal back, Nancy held out a creamy satin dress with rhinestones dancing over the neck and shoulders. "Check this one

71

out," she said with a wry grin. "It's for Heather Richards."

"Ugh," snorted Bess. "It'll look great on her, too."

"Here's Natasha's," Nancy said, reaching for a forest-green velvet gown.

"Are those ruffles on the front?" Bess asked.

"I don't know," Nancy answered, lifting up the plastic to check it out.

The answer was all too clear as soon as the cover was off the gown. The material was hanging in long, jagged shreds. Natasha's designer creation had been slashed to pieces!

Chapter

Eight

Fingering the shredded remains of Natasha's gown, Nancy said, "She'll never be able to wear this!"

The delivery boy walked over to make his own inspection. "All I did was pick these up from Smash and bring them here," he said.

"Did you leave the gowns alone at any point?" Nancy asked the boy.

He thought for a moment before clapping a hand to his forehead. "I had a message waiting for me when I got here," he told Nancy. "It said to call my office immediately. I left the rack alone for about five minutes while I made the call. The funny thing was, no one at the office knew who had left that message!"

Nancy nodded. The saboteur had struck again. And once again, no one had seen him—or her.

"You're not going to get in trouble over this, are you?" Bess asked the delivery boy.

"No way," he said. "My boss knows he can trust me. But I'd better phone and tell him there's a problem." He nodded and waved goodbye.

Bess turned to Nancy. "What in the world is going on?"

Nancy met Bess's bewildered expression seriously. "I don't know, Bess," she said, guiding her friend into the elevator. "But I intend to find out."

"Sounds like a mystery to me," Bess commented knowingly.

"Excuse me. I understand you gave a message a while ago to the boy who was delivering dresses for the Face of the Year contest," Nancy said to the young woman behind the counter in the lobby.

The girl blinked. "So I did," she said with a

little laugh. "I remember the delivery boy because I was dying to get a peek at those gowns!"

Nancy grinned. "I know what you mean. You
don't by any chance remember who left the
message for him, do you? Was it a man or a
woman?"

"I really don't. Sorry."

"Thanks anyway," Nancy said. She turned to
Bess. "Another dead end. Come on, I'll fill you in
while we eat."

"I'm really not hungry anymore," Bess said as
they took seats in a booth and opened their
menus. "I mean, this contest is too weird."

"Hi. What can I get you?" asked a perky
waitress who walked up to them with her pad
open.

Bess ordered a baked apple and tea. Nancy
asked for an eclair. "Okay, Bess," she began after
the waitress had left, "as you know, funny things
have been going on. For instance—"

"Baked apple here." The waitress had come
back to the table and was setting down their
order.

"Thanks," Nancy and Bess told her.

Bess looked anxious. "For instance—what?"
she said. "Don't keep me in suspense, Nan! What
do you suspect?"

"All right," Nancy said. "It started with that first accident by the lake." As Bess listened raptly, Nancy filled her in on everything.

When she was finished, Bess shook her head sadly. "Oh, Nancy," she said, "what if—what if one of the models is trying to sabotage the contest? Someone like Heather Richards?"

Nancy carefully forked a piece of eclair and popped it into her mouth. Heather's hostility toward everyone in the contest made her an easy target of suspicion.

Bess set her fork down and leaned in toward Nancy. "Well, you've got to admit that *she* hasn't had the least little problem! Maggie Adams got dumped in the lake, Alison Williams got her hair frizzed, Natasha's dress got shredded, *I* got a mud bath. Dear old Heather has just sailed through the contest making cracks about everybody else."

"I hear you, Bess," Nancy said. "But remember, there are a few other girls who haven't had anything bad happen to them either—Carey and Trudy and Diana."

"Nancy, Carey Harper is the sweetest girl in the world!" Bess protested. "As for Trudy and Diana—why, those girls wouldn't hurt a fly!"

"I'm not saying they would, Bess. I'm just trying to be logical. I'm not saying Heather isn't a good suspect—she is. But she's not the only one."

"I know it's Heather," Bess murmured.

"What about Roger Harlan?" Nancy asked. She reached for her water and took a sip before going on. "I'm pretty sure that tie tack is his. What I can't figure out is what his motive would be. I'm going to try to find out more about him tomorrow."

Just then the waitress appeared holding a pot of hot water. "More tea?" she asked.

"Not for me. You can take this away, though," Nancy said, pointing to her half-eaten eclair.

"Was there something wrong with it?" the waitress asked.

"No," Nancy replied, surprised. "I've just had enough."

"I hate you, Drew," Bess said. "I mean, 'enough eclair.' There's no such thing!"

"Just think about how great that size-four gown is going to look on you, Bess," Nancy reasoned.

"True, true." Bess sighed and smiled. "And who knows, maybe it will be love at first sight for me and Ernest Mullins. Ernest Mullins and Bess Marvin. Hey! If we get married, I won't even have to change my initials!"

Nancy rolled her eyes. "It's after six," she said,

glancing up at the sleek black clock over the cashier's station. "You'd better go get ready."

"I know," Bess said, standing up. "My new makeup routine takes an hour! Oh, Nancy," she added with a sad sigh, "maybe we're wrong. Maybe all these terrible incidents have just been accidents—a run of bad luck."

"Maybe." In her heart, Nancy didn't believe it, and neither, she knew, did Bess.

"Guess what?" Maggie Adams greeted them as they stepped off the elevator. "Our dresses are here!" She was standing in the hall with Trudy, Carey, Diana, and Natasha.

"Jackie told us to pick them up right away. So come on!" Trudy pulled Bess gently by the arm.

"Wait till you see mine," Natasha gushed in her melodious accent. "It's the deepest and lushest forest green."

Bess and Nancy couldn't help but exchange a quick glance. They said nothing as they walked into the Smash suite. Nancy had decided not to report what she knew about the dress so maybe she could learn something from people's reactions.

"This is so exciting!" Diana said, clapping her hands.

"I know," Carey added, beaming.

Bettina's assistant, Jackie, was standing next to
the rack. "Here they are," she announced. Nancy
stepped back as Heather Richards walked into
the room.

"I see mine! I see mine!" Diana Amsterdam
said, pointing to the first dress on the rack.

"Ooooh!" the girls cooed as the assistant
handed Diana her dress. It was pink silk with a
single white rose embroidered on the front.

"Maggie Adams?" the assistant asked.

Beaming, Maggie stepped back from the rack
and twirled around, holding her peach dress up
to her lithe figure. "Isn't it gorgeous?" she asked.

"It's beautiful," Nancy answered, returning
Maggie's contagious smile.

"Is Alison Williams here?" Jackie asked.

A murmur swept through the group. "She's
still in her room," Trudy said. "Maybe I can
bring it to her."

"That's okay," announced a voice behind
them. Alison Williams walked proudly into the
suite and reached for a deep blue gown. On her
head was a wig of lustrous, natural-looking hair.
"Thank you."

Trudy Woo ran over and hugged Alison. "You
look fantastic, Allie!"

"Monique got it for me," Alison explained.

"Natasha?" Jackie called out.

Nancy winced as the tall brunette stepped up to the rack. "I am here!" Natasha cried.

Without looking at the gown she was holding, Jackie handed it to the model.

"That's a strange design," Heather Richards said snidely as Natasha lifted the plastic to examine the dress more closely.

"Oh, no!" Natasha gasped. "It's ruined!"

Everyone moaned—everyone except Heather, who ignored Natasha as she reached for her own gown.

Obviously satisfied, the tall blonde took the creamy satin dress and sauntered out of the suite with it. The other contestants gathered around Natasha, trying to comfort her.

"I'll call Bettina right away," Jackie said, picking up the phone.

"I saw Thom Fortner in the hall a couple of minutes ago," Alison said. "Maybe he can help."

Nancy walked to the door and peeked out. About thirty feet down the hall, Heather was showing Thom her ball gown.

"There's a problem," Nancy announced. "Thom, could you come here a minute?"

Thom looked up. "Excuse me, Heather," he said. "Nothing serious, I hope," he said to Nancy.

"Well . . ." Nancy hedged. "You can judge for yourself."

The minute Thom stepped into the room, the other models swarmed around him.

"Natasha's dress is in shreds!" Carey Harper exclaimed, leading him over to Natasha, who was sitting in a chair, sobbing.

"I just called Bettina. She's on her way. There it is," Jackie said, pointing to the dress that was draped over her desk. Thom bent over to inspect it as the girls crowded around him.

Nancy stepped back out of the way. That was how she saw the small piece of paper that fell out of Thom's pocket when he leaned over the desk to inspect the dress.

"Do you have any idea how this happened?" he asked Natasha.

"It wasn't her fault," Bess said quickly. "The dress was ruined when she got it off the rack!"

Nancy edged over to the desk. Jackie was behind it, but she was watching Thom and the girls. Nancy kept her eyes on them, too, but she managed to knock over a pencil holder with her elbow.

"Oh, sorry!" Nancy said as the pencils crashed to the floor. "I'll pick them up."

No one was paying the least bit of attention to

her as she squatted down. As she did, she deftly
fingered open the paper Thom had dropped.

I'll miss you tonight. But remember, your
first reward will be a trip to the Caribbean,
with your new president, of course.

With love,
T.

Chapter

Nine

NANCY QUICKLY PUT the note in her pocket and scrambled to her feet. *T* had to be a woman, she surmised. Only a woman would sign a note to a man "with love." But who was she? And to what "new president" did the note refer? Nancy was certain the reference was not to politics.

A voice at the door broke her concentration. "What is it *this* time?" Bettina Vasquez was walking into the room with a look of extreme irritation on her face.

"You're not going to like this," Thom said, handing her the shredded dress.

"Oh, dear," the Elan executive said as she fingered the material. "Well, Natasha, I can get you another dress to wear tonight, but I'm afraid you won't be in any of the shots."

"No!" Natasha protested. "But it wasn't my fault!"

"Sorry," Bettina said, without a lot of feeling. "These gowns are each one of a kind. We simply can't include one that's not a Smash original."

Natasha's lip trembled and her chin quivered, but she said nothing.

"I can't think who'd do this. It's rotten," Bettina said a little more softly. "But those are the breaks."

Nancy scowled. Personally, she could think of a *few* people who might have done it—Bettina Vasquez among them. How else could Bettina's cool indifference be explained?

"Now, girls"—Bettina turned to the others—"not a word about this to anyone. If the press got hold of this story, it would be the end of the Face of the Year Contest. Understand?"

Nancy couldn't tell whether the contestants understood or not, but one thing was clear. All of them were terribly upset by the suspicious events surrounding their contest.

Over the next hour and a half they all tried hard to forget Natasha's dress as they concentrated on getting ready for the banquet. The sounds of unhappy murmuring were gradually replaced by giggling as the girls dashed from room to room borrowing hair clips and perfume or sharing makeup tips. Bess and Nancy's room had turned into a hub of activity.

Natasha was there, wearing a simple mint-green dress she'd been given. Nancy couldn't help thinking that even though she looked lovely in it, the new dress was no match for the color of the designer original.

"Remember, Natasha," Maggie Adams said as she helped Bess step into her filmy blue creation, "being out of just one shoot isn't going to ruin your chances of winning the contest. That's what Bettina told me when I couldn't be in the 'Welcome to Chicago' shot."

"And I never made it into the sportswear shoot," Bess added.

"I missed the group shot of the makeover," Alison Williams said.

"Oh, I hope you're right," Natasha said with a sigh.

"Girls! Girls!" Bettina called from the corridor. "I'm going downstairs to help set up, but I want you all to be in the lobby with Jackie by seven forty-five—sharp!"

"It's almost time to go!" Bess squealed as Maggie zipped up her gown. "How do I look, Nan?"

"Great!" Nancy said, reaching for her camera. "Can I get a quick shot of you all?"

"Sure!"

All the girls beamed as they shrieked, "Cheese!"

When Nancy put the camera down, Bess went to the bureau to pick up her white sequined bag and check her makeup one last time. "Oh, if only I looked like this every day," she said.

"Nobody looks like that every day, Bess," Nancy replied with a smile.

"Not even the most beautiful women in the world," Maggie Adams agreed.

"You know something? Being beautiful is really hard work," Diana added with a giggle.

"Let's go, everyone!" Jackie called in from the hallway. "An elevator's coming!"

When Nancy and the others stepped into the corridor, they saw the rest of the contestants, who all began oohing and aahing over one another's fabulous dresses. Even Nancy got a few compliments on her sleek black dress with rhinestone buttons that went down the back.

"Where's Heather?" Jackie asked.

"She went down a few minutes ago," Carey answered.

Jackie shrugged, and the elevator doors swept open. Nancy waited for the girls to step in. Because of the full skirts on some of their gowns, the models took up more room than usual. The elevator was packed.

"You go ahead. I'll meet you downstairs," Nancy called to Bess as the elevator doors were sliding shut.

Nancy looked up at the floor indicator and noticed that the other elevators were all on high floors. She decided to take the stairs down the three flights from the fourth floor.

As she headed down to the far end of the corridor where the door to the stairwell was located, her eyes widened in surprise. Bettina Vasquez was slipping furtively through the door marked Fire Stairs.

Strange. Bettina had said she was going to the ballroom a little while ago.

When the fire stairs door swung shut, Nancy ran over to it and listened. She could hear the sharp rap of Bettina's heels as she ran down the stairs.

Slipping off her black pumps, Nancy eased the door open quietly and stepped inside.

Bettina was talking to someone on the stairs below.

"And when I looked at it," Bettina was saying in hushed tones, "the gown had been slashed to ribbons. I tell you, it's *sabotage,* pure and simple. And I can promise you this—*it's going to happen again!"*

Holding her breath, Nancy tiptoed lightly down another step or two. Maybe if she could reach the next landing, she'd be able to see who Bettina was talking to.

"Well," Bettina went on with a laugh. "Do you have enough?"

"Yes, definitely," answered a male voice. From the sound of it, Nancy guessed the speaker was an older man. "And here's something for your trouble. Keep me in mind if you find out anything more."

The light rustling of paper alerted Nancy to the fact that Bettina was being paid for what she knew.

"You know, you really don't have to give me anything," Bettina purred. "Anything that reflects badly on Elan is payment enough."

The man chuckled. "Buy yourself a little something," he said.

"Well, if you insist," Bettina replied with a little laugh. "Thanks, E.B. Shall we go?"

With that, Nancy heard the click of Bettina's heels and the creak of a door opening. Nancy tore down another flight, but before she could see E.B., he and Bettina were gone.

Pounding down the last stairs, Nancy threw open the fire door. The long carpeted hallway of the second floor was deserted in both directions. She'd lost them—for the time being, at least. Her shoes still in hand, Nancy thought about what she'd just heard.

It's sabotage, Bettina had said, and it's going to happen again.

How can she be so sure? Nancy wondered. Unless she's causing the sabotage herself.

Chapter

Ten

NANCY EXPECTED TO SEE Bess and the other contestants the minute she stepped into the banquet hall. Under the crystal chandeliers, the room was abuzz with guests and waiters and waitresses flitting around.

But the only contestant Nancy saw was Heather Richards. She was sitting at the long rectangular table set up on a platform in the front of the hall. Roger Harlan, devastating in a crisp white shirt and black tuxedo, sat beside her, looking uncomfortable. Heather was pressed close to him, keeping up a steady stream of talk.

At the same head table were seven other young men in formal wear—the Elan models who were to escort the Face of the Year contestants. They kept glancing at the entrance, and from the expressions on their faces, Nancy could tell they, too, were wondering where the girls were.

Behind the head table, Thom Fortner was standing beside Monique Durand. Both were frowning.

"Nancy!"

Nancy whirled around to see Kelly waving to her from the service door. Kelly threw up her hands in a questioning gesture and hurried over to Nancy.

"The whole fashion industry is arriving, and nobody can find the girls!" Kelly lamented.

"They were in the elevator on their way down at least fifteen minutes ago," Nancy said, surprised.

Kelly nervously fingered the collar of her blue satin blouse. "Well, they're not here yet."

"I don't see Bettina either," Nancy said, scanning the room again. She felt a growing sense of alarm.

"She was here a minute ago. I think she's in the

ladies' room now," Kelly replied. "I wish I knew what was going on."

"I don't like any of this," Nancy said. "In fact, I'm going to check out the elevators."

Nancy walked out of the ballroom into the lobby, heading for the elevators, but she hadn't gotten far when she heard and saw seven severely shaken females.

"I was so scared!" Trudy Woo was saying. "I thought we were going to *die* in there!"

"Nancy! Nancy!" Bess cried, running up to her with eyes wide. "Am I ever glad to see you!"

"Me, too!" Nancy said, returning Bess's hug. "What happened?"

"We were trapped in the elevator," Bess told her. "A couple of seconds after we got in, the lights went out, and then we just *sat* there!"

"It felt like hours!" Alison added.

"How *did* you get out?" Nancy asked.

Bess shrugged. "The elevator just started working again."

"Well, we were all worried about you," Nancy told them. "Your escorts are here, and so are the media, and people from the fashion industry. They're all waiting inside."

The girls hurried toward the banquet hall with Nancy following.

"You made it!" Kelly said as they stepped inside. She nodded to Nancy and grinned. "I saved two seats for us at a table up front."

Just outside the banquet hall a hand clutched Nancy's arm. "Nancy, I see Ernest Mullins!" Bess whispered excitedly. "He's sitting two seats away from Roger Harlan, on the left." Ernest had chestnut hair and deep-set eyes. Even from where she stood, Nancy could see the dimple in his chin that Bess said had made him so famous.

"Better go inside and meet him, Bess," Nancy said, giving her friend a gentle push. "I'm not going to sit down just yet."

Bess turned back to Nancy with a questioning look. "Where are you going? Are you going to investigate something? Need any help?"

Nancy let out a little laugh. "Forget it, Bess. Your job is to look beautiful and have a good time tonight."

Bess shrugged her shoulders and joined the line of girls as they got ready to make their entrance. Heather had come out to join them.

"How about me?" Kelly asked after the girls entered the ballroom to oohs and aahs and applause. "Can I help?"

"I'd rather you stay here and keep an eye on things," Nancy said. "I don't think I'll be long."

Nancy headed for the elevator and got in. Pressing a button, she made her way to the hotel basement.

The doors opened on an underground world—the hidden underbelly of the hotel. Here were all the power and supplies needed to keep the guests comfortable.

When Nancy stepped out, she saw a man in a green maintenance uniform. "Do you know anything about an elevator breakdown?" she asked.

"I sure do," he said, pointing to a huge control board on the other side of the corridor. "It happened right here. I was on my dinner break, and somebody pushed this circuit breaker."

"Who'd do a thing like that?" Nancy asked.

"That's what I'm wondering. We don't usually have people pulling pranks around here." He shrugged his shoulders. "But anybody could have gotten here—just like you did. Tomorrow I get a lock for this board."

"Thanks," Nancy told him. "I appreciate your showing me."

When Nancy reentered the banquet hall, Kelly instantly asked, "Find anything out?"

Nancy filled her in. While she was at it, she took out the note that had fallen from Thom Fortner's pocket and handed it to Kelly.

"'I'll miss you tonight,'" Kelly read out loud.

"So whoever wrote this note isn't here. 'Your new president.' What new president?"

"That's what I'd like to know," Nancy said.

"By the way," Kelly said, handing Nancy the note, "see the gray-haired man with the red bow tie?" She nodded in the direction of the press, two tables away. "That's Earl Banks, the gossip columnist."

"Earl Banks—E.B.," Nancy murmured, thinking about what she'd heard in the stairwell.

"Right," Kelly said. "That's what they call him. He'd love to get something nasty to write about this contest, you know."

"Why?" Nancy asked.

"E.B. has two jobs. He writes his regular column. And he also writes copy for Let's Go, Trina Evans's clothing company," Kelly explained. "Whenever he can hurt Smash, he does."

"Wow," Nancy said. "They really play hardball in the fashion business, don't they?"

"You got it," Kelly said.

"E.B. and Bettina had a private chat not too long ago," Nancy began, filling Kelly in on the conversation she'd heard in the stairwell.

When the waiter came with their dinners, Nancy's gaze flicked up to the platform. Ernest Mullins was leaning over Maggie, talking to

Roger. Bess caught Nancy's eye. She rolled her eyes subtly to the ceiling. "Boring," she mouthed, pointing inconspicuously at Ernest.

Nancy smiled and shrugged, and a playful grin came over Bess's face. She shrugged lightly, too, to show that she accepted her fate. She was still going to have fun at the banquet.

After dinner Thom Fortner received an award from the Chamber of Commerce. For bringing the Face of the Year to Chicago, Thom deserved the thanks of the whole city, the chamber speaker said.

Then there was a photo session with the models on a small runway. Everyone could watch the girls and their escorts having their pictures taken.

The Smash designers were introduced last, and the ceremonies were over by about ten-thirty. Nancy and Kelly stepped up onto the runway with a few of the other contestants' friends after the girls and their escorts were done.

"A bunch of them are going out to Zero Hour, the music club," Bess said, walking over to Nancy. "They want me to go, too."

"Sounds like fun, Bess," Nancy commented. "Even if your date isn't the most exciting guy in the world, you'd have a chance to dance and cut loose a little."

Bess's face grew serious. "Nancy, I can't think about having fun," she protested. "Not if I'm going to win this contest. I'm meeting Alex Bogorofsky tomorrow morning, remember? I've got to look my best."

There was no doubt about it, Nancy thought, Bess wanted to be the Face of the Year more than anything. Despite the tension surrounding the contest, she was committed to doing her absolute best. That made Nancy proud. It also made her determined.

If Bess was going to fight hard to win, Nancy was going to fight just as hard—to make sure the contest was fair.

"Be it ever so humble, there's no place like my cubicle," Kelly joked as she led Nancy into the small partitioned office that was part of the larger offices of *Teen Scene* magazine. The reporter had invited Nancy to stop by so they could look at the morning papers together and see what Earl Banks and the other columnists were saying about Face of the Year.

"This is definitely the desk of a busy person," Nancy remarked. Papers, pencils, and an open container of spring water were scattered across the top.

"All I really need is my computer and a phone," Kelly explained, walking behind the desk, pulling out her chair, and sitting down.

"So. Any word about Heather?" Nancy asked, sitting in the chair next to Kelly's desk.

"Not yet. But I have feelers out."

A knock on the cubicle wall interrupted them. "Got your papers, Kelly," said a short man who tossed a pile of newspapers onto Kelly's small desk.

"Thanks, Fred," Kelly yelled, but he was already gone.

"I can't wait to see what Earl Banks said about the contest," Kelly said, thumbing through a paper.

Nancy watched as Kelly's eyes widened. She smoothed out the paper and said, "Nancy, listen to this. 'Smash calls it the Face of the Year, and let me tell you, Chicago, this face needs a lift. Oh, the girls are pretty enough, and the clothes are cute. But word has it that some nasty little gremlin is doing everything he or she can to make sure the face gets plenty of worry lines and wrinkles before its time. Did I say *sabotage?* Of a beauty contest? My, my, what will they think of next. . . .'"

Kelly closed the paper with a sigh. "It's

strange," she said. "Bettina was the one who said the girls had to be quiet about the contest problems. She obviously didn't take her own advice."

Nancy began tapping her fingers on Kelly's desk. "Kelly, let's go back to the beginning for a minute. Why would anybody want to sabotage something as innocent as this contest?"

Kelly let out a breath in a single loud puff. "Well, it could just be personal. You know, one individual trying to hurt another individual—"

"Right, like Bettina trying to hurt Monique by hurting Elan," Nancy suggested.

"Right, or Roger Harlan trying to make Elan look bad so he can get out of his contract—"

"But what if it's *not* personal?" Nancy asked. "Why else would anyone be interested in sabotaging this contest?"

"Nancy, there's a lot of money in the rag trade, as we call the clothing business. Millions—no, *billions*—of dollars are spent on clothes every year, and competition between the major producers can get pretty ugly."

"You're saying rival companies may resent all the publicity Smash is getting from the Face of the Year contest?" Nancy asked. "Then maybe they want to make sure a good portion of that publicity is bad."

Kelly nodded thoughtfully. "But Smash and Elan are keeping such a tight rein on the contest. Only their people are anywhere near it."

Nancy looked over at Kelly. "Corporate war is a fact of life, isn't it? Maybe another clothing company has an employee on the staff at Smash."

Kelly's green eyes widened. "You may have something there, Nancy. Hmmm . . ."

The phone rang, and Kelly held up a hand to signal Nancy to wait while she answered. "Thanks for letting me know. I'll be there right away." Kelly put the phone down. "The Chicago Bears are going to be at the airport in twenty minutes, and I've got to go interview them. They're serious superhunks, Nancy. Want to come?"

Tempted, Nancy considered briefly, then shook her head. "I can't," she answered. "Bess may need me."

"Now that's what I call true friendship," Kelly said with a laugh as she stood up and grabbed a raincoat from a nearby coat rack.

Nancy decided to walk back to the hotel. On the way, she passed a large pharmacy and stopped in to see if they had Heavenly Pink nail polish. They did.

Nancy bought a bottle and smiled as she tucked it into her pocket. Bess would be pleased.

But when Nancy got back to the hotel and up to her room, she knew that nail polish wasn't going to help. The moment she stepped up to the door to put her key in, she could hear Bess sobbing inside.

"Bess!" Nancy cried as she opened the door and saw her friend's tearstained face. Rivulets of teal-blue mascara ran down her flushed cheeks, and her eyes were all red and puffy.

Bess glanced up for a moment, then buried her face in the pillow she was clutching. "Oh, Nancy. My life is over!" she wailed.

"What happened?" Nancy asked, going to the bed and sitting down beside her.

Bess lifted her head and said, between sobs, "Alex Bogorofsky said I was st-st-stiff and phony, and that I'd never make it as a model."

"But, Bess," Nancy said, gently stroking her friend's back, "that's ridiculous! I saw the pictures that George took of you, and they were great! You didn't look stiff at all!"

"That's because I was with George," Bess moaned. "With her I was relaxed. But Bogorofsky made me tense. The minute I walked into his studio he said, 'What is this? A circus shoot? You look like a clown—go wash your face.' He hated me!"

"I'm sure you're exaggerating, Bess," Nancy

said gently. "And besides, you said yourself Bogorofsky's known for photographing the essence of a person. He probably wanted you to start fresh so that he could get pictures of you that were really unique."

Bess nodded thoughtfully. "That could be true."

"For all you know, those were the best photos ever taken of you," Nancy added. "Bogorofsky is one of the greatest photographers in the world, right?"

A small smile began to play on Bess's lips. "He did smile at me at the very end. When he said, 'Zank goodness, we're through.'"

A knock on the door interrupted them.

"Bess, it's me, Thom Fortner."

"Oh, no, and look at me," Bess whispered to Nancy. "Coming!" she called out loudly. She raced to the bathroom and slapped some clean water on her face. Then Nancy held out a pair of sunglasses for Bess to put on so the P.R. man wouldn't notice that she'd been crying.

"Hi, Thom," Bess purred as she cracked the door open. "What is it?"

Thom bit his lip. "Sorry to be the bearer of bad news," he said, "but I just spoke to Alex Bogorofsky a few minutes ago. The camera he took your pictures with was stolen—along with all your negatives."

Bess swallowed hard. "My negatives are g-gone?"

Suddenly Bess had forgotten how badly her session had gone. Nancy stepped over to stand beside her trembling friend.

"You mean I won't get to have a portrait?" Bess asked in a quavering voice.

"I'm terribly sorry," Thom said, coming into the room. "But there's nothing I can do."

Nancy knew what her friend was thinking—without those pictures she had no chance of winning the contest!

Chapter

Eleven

Nancy strode up to Thom. "Where was the camera stolen from?" she asked.

Thom looked puzzled. "I'm not sure. I believe it was left at the studio or something. In any case, the odds of its being recovered are extremely slim."

"Well, there's got to be something we can do," Nancy insisted. "Can't Bess have the pictures reshot?"

Fortner turned to Bess and took her hand.

"Well, I suppose we could try to get you another session with Bogorofsky."

"You mean you might not be able to?" Bess moaned.

"Even if it can be arranged, you'd have to miss one of the group shots," Thom said.

"But I already missed one!" Bess protested.

"Now, let's not get all upset," Thom said in a soothing tone of voice. "Tell you what. Bogorofsky is going to be at the sundress shoot this afternoon. We'll talk to him then." Squeezing her hand, he turned to walk out the door.

"That guy is creepy," Bess said after he'd gone. "I know he's trying to be nice, but he seems phony."

"I know," Nancy agreed. "Come on, let's go to lunch," she suggested.

"Okay," Bess said with a resigned sigh. "My stomach was growling all morning. It growled during my photo session. Fortunately, Bogorofsky thought it was *his* stomach. He said, 'Excuse, I have pizza yesterday.'"

Most of the other models were already eating lunch. "Don't let me order anything fattening," Bess said to Nancy as they stepped in.

"I won't," Nancy said. "I'd like to sit with Heather, if that's okay with you. I want to get to know her better."

"Being with Heather will ruin my appetite for sure. Hmmm . . ." Bess smiled ironically. "The Heather Richards diet. I think I'm onto something."

"Are these seats free?" Nancy asked Heather when they came up beside her.

"I guess so," Heather said with a shrug.

Nancy and Bess sat down, and Heather continued eating her lobster salad.

"That looks good," Bess said, trying to be polite. "I think I'll order one."

"The waiter told me it was the last one," Heather said with a look of false regret. "Sorry."

"Oh, well," Bess said with a sigh, looking over the menu the waiter had just brought to the table.

"Achoo!" came a volcanic eruption behind her.

"Hi, Maggie!" Bess said brightly. "Want to join us?"

"Achoo!" Maggie let out another gigantic sneeze and nodded her head affirmatively. "Thanks," she murmured. "Sorry about the—*achoo!*—sneezing."

Heather rolled her eyes to the ceiling. "I hope whatever you have isn't catching," she said icily. "Have you seen a doctor?"

"No, it's just a little cold," Maggie said, embarrassed.

"Well, being in the contest may make it

worse," Heather went on, her voice dripping with phony sympathy. "You know, if *I* were you, I'd think about dropping out so I could get some rest."

"Thanks for the suggestion, Heather. It's nice that you care," Maggie said, smiling through gritted teeth.

"Did you hear?" Bess began, in what Nancy guessed was an effort to change the subject. "My photo negatives were stolen!"

"Oh, no!" Maggie moaned. "That's awful, Bess! What's going to happen?"

"They're going to try to get me another session with Bogorofsky," Bess explained.

"But the first session with any photographer is always the best," Heather said. "You can redo them, but they're never as good as the first ones."

"Really?" Bess asked.

"Everyone knows that," Heather said. "See you at Grant Park." She pushed her plate away and stood up.

After the icy blonde left the table, Maggie, Bess, and Nancy sat in silence.

"Achoo." That was all they needed. Suddenly all three of them were giggling their heads off. "Nothing like a good sneeze to get rid of tension," Maggie managed to say.

* * *

The weather had turned warmer that afternoon when the girls arrived at Buckingham Fountain in Grant Park. Nancy had leads to investigate, but she was afraid the saboteur might try something that afternoon. She wanted to be on hand in case she could help.

Jackie told them that the three-tiered marble fountain was a larger replica of one in the gardens at Versailles in France. The pool around the fountain had been drained. The water was shut off until the girls were ready to take their positions on the pedestals that were part of the design. After a few shots, they'd be given umbrellas and the fountain would be turned on.

After Jackie directed the models to the trailer, Nancy walked over to where the crew was setting up. Bogorofsky was wandering around, snapping candids, until the lights were ready.

Nancy noticed Thom Fortner at the far side of the fountain. He was wearing a navy coat with a fur collar and carrying his ever-present briefcase. Thom saw Nancy and gave a stiff wave. Then he turned, and Nancy lost sight of him.

Not far from the trailer was Bettina. She was talking to the news reporter Nancy had first seen on the pier. Nancy wondered if Bettina was dishing more dirt about the contest. As if to confirm Nancy's suspicions, Bettina moved away from the reporter when she saw Nancy. Seconds later she was clapping her hands for attention. "Let's get started, please!" she announced. "Would someone please see if the girls are ready?"

"I will," Nancy offered with a smile.

Nancy walked over and poked her head in the door of the trailer. "Are you ready?" she asked.

"Almost," Bess called out. A wardrobe mistress was busy pinning Bess's dress in the back. "It's the wrong size," Bess explained. "All the dresses were—except one!"

"Don't worry," the wardrobe mistress muttered, taking a pin from her mouth. "They'll look fine."

"What do you think?" Heather Richards asked sweetly, twirling around in a tomato-red sundress that fit perfectly and showed off her slender shoulders and narrow waist.

"Honey, you sure you're not a pro?" the wardrobe mistress joked.

Heather seemed momentarily taken aback. "No! Of course not! Professionals aren't eligible for this contest!"

"I just meant that you look great, that's all," the wardrobe lady explained. "Let's go, everyone!"

One by one the girls stepped past Nancy and

walked out of the trailer. From the front they looked fine, but in the back their dresses were clipped with safety pins.

Trudy Woo watched Heather in bright red step down and let out a growl. "How does she do it?" Trudy asked.

"Heather's the one behind everything. Trust me," Bess whispered to Nancy.

"You've got to be able to prove these things, Bess," Nancy reminded her.

Nancy watched the trail of girls cross the drained pool to take their positions standing on the pedestals of the fountain.

"The red dress is offensive and out of place!" Bogorofsky complained to Bettina.

"That's the way Smash wants it," Bettina said with a shrug. "They're paying for the shoot today."

"Ridiculous," the photographer said. "But what do I know? I'm only an artist. All right, young lady in red, move to the pedestal down front, in the center."

After Bogorofsky had taken a series of shots, he waved to the crew, who were waiting at the edge of the pool with umbrellas. "I'm ready for you," the photographer said.

The crew handed each of the models an umbrella. The umbrellas were all made of shiny vinyl in bright, bold colors. At least in this round of photos Heather wouldn't stand out as much, Nancy thought.

"All right! Let's do it," Bogorofsky shouted. "Where's the water?" he yelled, looking up again.

"Coming! We just found the mechanism to turn it on."

"Let's have it, then!" Bogorofsky shouted. Instantly the fountain began spraying far up into the air.

Something was terribly wrong. The water coming out of the fountain was a deep, ugly purple! It showered all over the girls, who began shrieking hysterically.

Thom Fortner's jaw dropped open. "B-but— but," he sputtered, "that's not water—it's paint!"

Chapter

Twelve

SCREAMS FILLED THE AIR as the shower of purple liquid rained down on the models who stood on the upper pedestals. Since the wind blew the fountain's jets away from the girls down in front—including Heather—they avoided getting splattered.

In seconds the crew had the fountain shut off, but the damage to Smash's sundresses, and to the shoot, was already done. Nancy let out a little gasp as she caught sight of Bess's paint-streaked face.

"What happened?" Thom Fortner cried out.

"What kind of prank is this?" a furious Bettina shouted at the bewildered crew.

"I just hit the switch marked Fountain," Pat tried to explain.

"Oh, shut up," snapped Bettina. "What's the good of explanations now? This shoot is ruined!"

One by one the paint-spattered models got off their pedestals and walked to the trailer.

"I quit!" Bogorofsky fumed after making sure none of the purple spray had gotten on his lenses.

So much for Bess's portfolio, Nancy thought sadly.

"These pictures will be even better than the ones I took when the girl was dumped in the lake!" The same reporter had popped up once again and was taking as many humiliating shots of the models as he could before they disappeared into their trailer.

While Bess and the others washed up and changed, Nancy checked out the back of the fountain to see what had happened.

A small metal box was sticking out from under a pedestal. Nancy guessed it was the fountain mechanism that Pat had been talking about. The top of the box was hinged. Inside, the levers that turned the fountain on and off were unbroken.

Bending down, Nancy peered around the box.

Hidden between it and the edge of the fountain was a transparent tube about a yard long. The tube was filled with purple paint. Reaching in, Nancy pulled on the tube. Something scraped along the ground toward her from under the fountain. A drum of paint! So somebody must have gotten there early and set up the mechanism. And whoever it was had to have done the dirty work after the fountain was shut off. In other words, not too long ago.

"What's that?" A voice behind Nancy startled her. She spun around to face Thom Fortner. How long had he been watching her?

"It's a drum of paint," Nancy told him. "See for yourself."

"You know, I thought all those rumors of sabotage were just so much nonsense," Thom murmured. "But I'm beginning to believe there's something to them after all."

Nancy didn't say anything—she wanted to see how Thom was going to respond to the situation.

"I hate to say it," Thom continued as he stood up, "but I think our only option at this point may be to cancel the contest."

Thom seemed to be giving up awfully easily.

"Come on, Nancy," Bess said, approaching Nancy. "Let's get back to the hotel so I can shower this disgusting stuff off. *If* it comes off."

Thom wandered over to Bettina as Nancy boarded the van with Bess and the other contestants.

Usually, when the group traveled somewhere, the trip was filled with the sounds of giggling, laughing, and high-spirited conversation. But that day the van made the short trip back to the hotel in dismal silence. Only Heather Richards, sitting alone in the front, seemed to be carefree.

The minute Nancy opened the door to their suite, she noticed the red message light on the phone flashing.

"I wonder who called," Bess said, her expression brightening a bit. "I love messages."

Nancy called down to the concierge. "Oh, yes, there were three calls for your suite," the woman told her. "Two for Bess Marvin, one from Thom Fortner and one from Leo Halsey." She gave Nancy the phone numbers and paused while Nancy wrote them down. "The other one is for Nancy Drew, from Kelly Conroy. She asks that Ms. Drew please call her immediately at *Teen Scene.*"

"Thanks," Nancy said, and hung up. She handed Bess her messages.

"Leo Halsey? Who's he?" Bess's brow wrinkled in puzzlement.

"You can find out in a minute. I want to catch

Kelly right away," Nancy said, dialing the switchboard at *Teen Scene.*

"Hi!" Kelly's voice bubbled.

"Hi," Nancy responded. "What's up?"

"Well," Kelly drawled dramatically, "sit down, 'cause you're going to love this. When I got back to the office this afternoon, my assistant had some news for me about Heather."

"Shoot," Nancy said, sitting down on the bed while Bess paced in front of her.

"First of all, her name isn't Heather Richards —it's Gloria Smithson."

"Keep going," Nancy said.

"And she's not from New York. She's from Cleveland, Ohio. *And* it seems she may have done some professional modeling, although there's no proof yet."

"Wow! That would disqualify her from the contest, wouldn't it?"

"You bet. *If* we can prove it. But that's not the best part."

"I'm listening," Nancy said.

"Here's the capper. Gloria was in a juvenile detention center a few months ago—for vandalism!"

"Good work, Kelly. Any news on Roger Harlan?"

"Just that he was an Eagle scout back in his hometown," Kelly said flatly. "Oh, and Monique mentioned that he's shooting a commercial at Marshall Field's tomorrow."

"Hmmm," Nancy said. "I think I'll go shopping. Let's get together afterward. I'll call you."

After Nancy hung up and relayed what she'd just learned to Bess, Bess exclaimed, "I knew it! Heather's responsible for the sabotage, Nancy!"

Nancy wasn't so sure. "Then tell me this, Bess," she said. "Why? Why is she out to sabotage a contest that could just possibly give her the one chance she needs to change her life?"

Bess bit her lip and shrugged her shoulders. "Beats me," she murmured.

"Your turn." Nancy handed her the phone.

"Hello, is Mr. Fortner there?" Bess said after she pressed in the number of Smash's executive offices.

Bess hung up a few minutes later. "He called to give me the name of my new photographer. That's who Leo Halsey is. I never heard of him. Thom says he does book covers."

"You sound disappointed," Nancy said gently.

"I am!" Bess agreed. "What a comedown! From Alex Bogorofsky to some unknown book-cover photographer. What an intense drag!"

"I thought you hated Bogorofsky."

"I did." Bess made a face. "But book covers? Honestly!"

Bess's mood hadn't improved much by morning. Dragging herself out of bed, she recited a litany of complaints as she got dressed. Everything was wrong—her hair, her face, her clothes.

"I don't have a chance of winning this contest," she began. "I mean, Leo Halsey? He's a complete unknown!"

"He must be good, Bess, if Smash and Elan are using him," Nancy suggested. "Why don't you give him a chance?"

Bess snorted derisively as she got ready for her appointment. "At least his studio is near the hotel," she said.

"There it is. Halsey, Studio Six," Bess muttered as they entered the tiny elevator that slowly delivered them to the sixth floor. "I hope he's not another prima donna. I don't think I could take it."

But when the door of the studio swung open, Nancy could tell that Bess's session was going to be fine. Leo Halsey was adorable. He was about twenty-four, with dark curly hair and light blue eyes.

"You're Bess," he said, grinning. "I'm Leo, and I'm going to take the pictures that are going to win you the Face of the Year Contest. Come on in. Let's relax and get to know each other before we start to work."

Bess beamed. Obviously she liked Halsey's approach—not to mention his good looks.

"I'm taking off," Nancy told Bess, who didn't seem to care much at that point.

"See you later, Nan," Bess said, vaguely waving goodbye as the door to the studio swung shut.

Nancy felt in her pocket for the gold tie tack she'd put there that morning. She was going to confront Roger Harlan. Taking the stairs instead of the elevator, Nancy let herself out of Leo's building and hurried over to Marshall Field's, which was just a few blocks away.

After she inquired about Roger's commercial, she was sent up to the fifth floor housewares department. As she rode the escalator up, she noticed someone familiar riding down beside her. It was Thom Fortner.

He acknowledged her with a quick wave, and Nancy waved back. With Thom was a willowy blonde with straight-cut bangs and deep green eyes. The woman was strangely familiar.

Nancy watched them as they rode down and

stepped off the escalator out of view. Nancy was left with the nagging thought that she'd seen that woman before.

But where?

Stepping off the escalator in the housewares department, Nancy made her way through towels and sheets. In an area roped off from the general public stood Roger Harlan, conferring with a man standing next to a huge camera on a dolly.

"I'm from Elan," Nancy fibbed as she approached the barriers separating the shoot from the rest of the store. A young woman holding a clipboard moved the chain away to let Nancy through.

"I need to talk to Roger Harlan when he's available," Nancy told her in a quiet tone.

"They should be breaking after a couple more takes," the woman whispered back.

"Okay, everyone!" the man Roger had been talking to called out loudly. "Let's take it again!"

"Marshall Field's, take forty-two," a young man with a chalkboard announced.

"You know, when I moved into my new apartment"—sounding nervous, Roger began walking slowly toward the camera—"I needed a few new things, so—"

"Cut!" the man behind the camera shouted.

"Roger, you've got to stay on your mark. Otherwise you won't be centered in the shot."

"No problem, Dan," Roger said as the makeup man redabbed his face.

"Let's try it again," the man said.

"Marshall Field's, take forty-three!" the man with the chalkboard said.

"You know," Roger began again, "when I moved into my new apartment, I—"

"Cut!" Dan shouted. "Make it more intimate, Roger. You're not talking to an acquaintance here. I want you to sound like you're talking to your best friend. Let your voice drop a little after that first 'you know.' I think that'll help."

"Marshall Field's, take forty-four!"

"You know," Roger began, stepping slowly toward the camera, "when I *moved* into my *new* apartment, I *needed* a few—"

"Cut!" the director shouted again.

By the time take fifty-seven was shot the director gave up and called a break. "But be back in ten," he announced. "Remember, this is only the first section."

"Roger," Nancy said, stepping up to the model, who looked absolutely drained. "I need to talk to you."

"Sure," he said, rubbing his shoulder as if it hurt. "What's up?"

121

Without fanfare Nancy removed the gold tie tack from her pocket and held it out to him. She watched his face closely for a reaction.

Roger broke into a huge smile. "My tie tack! Where'd you find it?" he said, taking the object and gazing at it fondly.

"Where did you lose it?" Nancy asked coolly.

"Beats me," Roger said. "I had it when I went to a fitting up at Smash, and the next time I looked for it, it was gone!"

Nancy looked straight into those often-photographed blue eyes and decided that he was telling the truth. There was an innocence there that couldn't be manufactured.

"Come on," he pressed her. "Tell me where you found it."

Quickly she filled him in on that, and on some of what had been going on in the contest. His eyes widened, first in shock, then in anger. "Nancy, if I can help you in any way, let me know."

The director was back on his feet, calling to the cast and crew. With a wave, Roger turned on his heel and went back to work.

Nancy watched until take sixty-two, then headed back to the hotel. Bess would probably still be at her session, and Nancy wanted some time alone. She needed to sort out her ideas about the case and decide what to do next.

When she stepped inside her hotel room, her eyes were immediately drawn to a piece of paper lying on her pillow. That's odd, Nancy thought. Bess was still gone, and any messages for them would've come to the front desk.

Nancy picked up the paper. In big block letters was a simple and direct message.

Nancy Drew, If you like your face the way it is, keep your nose out of other people's business.

Chapter

Thirteen

Nancy blinked and stared down at the note in her hands again. Receiving it was even more threatening, since its writer had managed to get into her room. Biting her lip, she thought of the bellhop who'd lost his passkey the other day. The author of this poisonous message had probably stolen the key.

The doorknob turned. Nancy's eyes flicked to it, her heart pounding. But when the door opened, she saw Bess, who sailed into the suite with a dreamy smile on her face.

"Nancy! I'm in love!" she announced. "Leo Halsey is the sweetest—I mean truly the sweetest, most adorable guy I have ever met in my entire life! He made me feel so comfortable and relaxed." She hugged herself blissfully. "Anyway, I just came back for lunch and to pick up some different clothes. Leo wants to do a whole spread of me as an old-fashioned eighteenth-century romantic. Long dresses and nosegays."

"Well, I'm really glad it worked out, Bess," she said.

"Okay." Bess's face grew serious. "What's wrong? I've known you for a long time, Nan, and I can tell when something's bothering you."

Nancy handed Bess the note without a word.

"Oh, no!" Bess cried after she read it. "This is horrible!"

"We've been in worse situations before, and I'm not going to give up now. I'm too close."

"Nancy, do you absolutely swear—I mean a truly solemn promise—to be careful? If anything happens to you, I'll never forgive myself! I'm the one who made you come here."

"Come on, Bess," Nancy said. "You know I'm always careful. Besides, nobody forced me to come here. I'm a big girl, and I make my own decisions."

"I still don't like it, Nan," she murmured.

"I'm not thrilled, either. But let's eat lunch," Nancy said, trying to sound light. "I'm hungry."

Bess gathered up some clothes and tossed them in the garment carrier that was a gift from Elan. "I guess I'm ready," she said, her spirit dampened by Nancy's note.

In the hotel café Trudy Woo, Maggie Adams, Alison Williams, and Natasha were all seated around a large table.

"Hi, guys, what's going on?" Bess asked, stepping up to the group.

"I have some news," Maggie said, looking up from her spinach salad. "I ran into Bettina this morning. She said she was able to persuade Alex Bogorofsky to stay in the contest! He won't do any more head shots, but he'll do the group shots, including the awards ceremony."

"That's good, I guess," Bess said.

"That's fantastic!" Alison said, far more enthusiastically. "Yesterday it looked like they were going to cancel the whole contest."

"Oh, no!" Trudy Woo let out a little cry. "Listen to this!" she said, holding up Earl Banks's column. "'As for the Farce of the Year Contest—oops, that's *Face* of the Year—look for an up-and-comer by the name of Heather Richards to walk away with the laurels. Though the contest has been a complete fiasco up to now, a little bird informs me that Heather's a fast runner, and she's already well positioned on the inside track. . . .'"

"I don't believe it," Maggie said, aghast.

"Something is very wrong with this whole contest," Natasha murmured.

"And I'd love to know who that 'little bird' is," Bess said.

Nancy wondered, too. Heather seemed to have Thom Fortner wrapped around her little finger, but it was Bettina Vasquez whom she'd heard talking to Earl Banks. Or maybe Heather was talking to reporters herself now.

"It kind of makes you want to give up, doesn't it?" Alison said with a disgusted look. "I mean, why bother competing if we don't have a chance?"

"I know," Natasha agreed. "It's really depressing." Silence fell over the group.

"Well, we're going to have lunch," Bess said. "Nothing like eating to make a person feel better. Even if it's only salad."

"You can sit here," Trudy said. "Natasha and I are leaving anyway."

"Where are Diana and Carey?" Nancy asked.

"Good question. They were going to sleep late, but this is ridiculous," Alison said, looking at her watch. "It's after one."

"Maybe one of us should go knock on their door," Maggie suggested.

"I can go," Nancy volunteered. "I have to go back to my room anyway. Bess, order me a grilled Swiss and tomato. I'll be right back."

Nancy stood up and walked out of the dining room. On the way to the fourth floor, she couldn't help thinking of Earl Banks's column. She was fairly sure that Bettina was the "little bird" Earl had written about. Dousing Elan with bad publicity had to be an evil thrill for Bettina, a way of soothing the hurt Monique had done to her heart.

But was Bettina setting Heather up to win? She didn't seem to like Heather. In fact, she enjoyed taking Heather down a peg or two sometimes.

Stepping off the elevator, Nancy noticed that the fourth floor was unusually quiet. Without the girls dashing through the halls, giggling and laughing or moaning about the way they looked, the place seemed dead.

Nancy went to her room and got her camera. Then she stepped down three doors and knocked on the door of the room that Carey and Diana shared.

"Hello?" Nancy called.

"Who's there?" Carey's voice sounded small and timid.

"It's me, Nancy."

"Oh, Nancy." Carey sounded relieved as she pulled open the door. "Look at my face!"

Nancy's eyes widened as she took in the huge blotches all over the aspiring model's face.

"Diana has it, too. She's in the bathroom, seeing if hot water will help it go away," Carey said, rubbing at her cheek. "It itches like crazy! We've tried astringent and cold cream, but they only made it worse."

"What is it?" Nancy asked. "An allergy?"

Carey looked helpless. "Neither one of us is allergic to anything. All we know is that when we woke up, we had it."

"Mind if I take a look at your pillow?" Nancy asked, playing a hunch.

"Sure, go ahead," Carey said, looking confused.

"We'll never be able to compete looking like this!" Diana moaned, coming out of the bathroom. Her face was full of blotches, too.

Nancy walked over to Carey's bed and ran her fingers over the pillow. Her fingers turned red instantly.

"I hate to tell you this," Nancy said, rubbing

her hands, "but someone put itching powder on your pillows."

"Oh, no!" Diana shrieked.

"What kind of powder?" Carey asked, a tremor in her voice.

"Well, I'm not sure," Nancy said, her fingers itching. "But if it's the usual kind of itching powder, it should stop driving you crazy in a couple of hours."

"A couple of hours?" Diana wailed.

"What about the red marks, Nancy?" Carey asked nervously.

"Sorry," Nancy said sympathetically. "They won't go away for days."

The two girls moaned miserably, and Nancy gritted her teeth. Somebody was doing an awfully good job of sabotaging this contest, and the contest was almost over. If she didn't solve this case soon, it would be too late!

Chapter

Fourteen

AFTER TRYING to soothe the feelings of the
blotchy-faced models, Nancy returned to the
dining room. Bess was still there, but Maggie and
the others had gone.

"Hi, Bess! Hi, Nancy!" Kelly called out just as
Nancy was sitting down. Kelly stepped up to the
table and pulled out a seat. Under her arm was a
slender, light gray briefcase that complemented
her periwinkle sweater and gray slacks. "What's
happening?" she asked.

Nancy took a breath and met Kelly's eyes. "I have some news," she began, and she filled Bess and Kelly in on what had happened to Carey and Diana.

"That's nasty stuff," Kelly said, shaking her head.

"I'll say!" Bess put in, being careful not to let her voice carry. "And whoever is causing all this trouble is trying to scare Nancy!"

"Is that true?" Kelly asked.

Nancy nodded reluctantly. "This was on my pillow this afternoon," she said, taking the note from her pocket and handing it to Kelly.

The reporter's eyes widened as she read the threat. "This is getting out of hand," she murmured.

"Oh—I'd like to get my hands on that Heather Richards," Bess hissed. "I just know she's behind everything!"

"Is that what you think, too, Nancy?" Kelly asked.

Nancy let out a sigh. "I think she may have something to do with what's going on," she said slowly, "but I'm not positive she wrote the note."

"Notice that Heather is always absent when trouble strikes?" Bess said, leaning toward them.

"She also has a busy schedule, Bess."

"Speaking of busy—yikes!" Bess cried, glancing at her wristwatch. "I'm supposed to be at Leo's right now!" She grabbed her handbag from the back of the chair.

"See you later," Nancy said, watching her friend fly out of the dining room with a quick wave.

After Bess was gone, Kelly turned to Nancy and said, "I found out something interesting. I was just at Elan and saw Heather there. Apparently Monique is already sending her out on go-sees."

"What are go-sees?" Nancy asked.

"That's when models go to see photographers about getting work," Kelly explained.

"But Heather hasn't even won the contest yet," Nancy pointed out. "The judges aren't voting until tonight."

Kelly shrugged. "I don't get it either. It seems pretty unfair to me."

"Come on, Kelly," Nancy said, standing up and taking her jacket off the back of her chair. "Let's go to Elan and see if Heather's still there. It's time to get to the bottom of this mess."

As the cab pulled up to the large office building, Nancy spotted Heather walking out.

"There she is," Nancy told Kelly. They scrambled out of the cab, chasing Heather as she walked. "Heather!" Nancy called out.

Heather turned around and waved but kept on walking.

"Heather! Wait!" Kelly cried.

"What do you want?" Heather snapped, and she continued walking. "I'm in a hurry!"

"We want to talk to you about something," Nancy told her. "It's important."

"I don't have time," Heather retorted.

"Then you'd better make time—*Gloria,*" Kelly said.

Heather stopped then and stared at the *Teen Scene* reporter. "How do you know my real name?" she asked.

"I know a lot of other things, too," Kelly said, her voice full of steel. "And so does Nancy."

"Come on," Nancy said more gently. "Let's find someplace to talk."

Heather stared at Nancy and Kelly, then glanced down at her wristwatch. "Let me make a call and tell the photographer I'll be late."

Kelly pulled some change out of her pocket. "Here," she said and she nodded at a nearby phone booth.

When Heather went to make her call, Nancy said, "This could be our break. Did you see the fear in her eyes just then?"

Kelly nodded somberly.

When Heather was done using the phone, she

pointed to a nearby bench. "We can talk there," she said in a subdued tone.

They sat down, and Heather turned to Nancy with a desperate look in her golden eyes. "If you're going to try to blackmail me," she said, "you should know that I don't have any money —not yet."

"We're not going to blackmail you," Nancy told her calmly. Funny, Nancy thought, how quickly Heather's mind had leapt to that conclusion. Is that what she would have done if their positions were reversed?

"We're not going to blackmail you, but we do want to know a few things," Kelly said.

"Such as?"

"Such as why you're the only contestant who hasn't been affected by any of the mishaps," Nancy said, leveling her gaze at Heather.

"Just luck, I guess." Heather gave a casual shrug, but her eyes showed how amused she was.

"What about the threatening note on Nancy's pillow?" Kelly blurted out.

Heather's eyes flickered with confusion for a minute, then set into a hard stare. "I don't know what you're talking about. I never wrote any note. And as far as I'm concerned, I haven't done anything wrong in a long time. It would be pretty rotten of you to tell people what you know."

"You say you haven't done anything wrong in a long time," Nancy said pointedly. "What about entering this contest even though you've worked as a professional model?"

Though Nancy didn't have hard proof, her wild shot hit home. Heather blinked and caught her breath momentarily, but in an instant her hard veneer was back in position. "You can't prove it," she said. "And besides," she added haughtily, "even if you *do* tell what you know, it won't matter."

"Think what you're doing, Heather," Nancy argued. "It won't do you any good to win the contest if Elan's reputation is ruined. They can't help your career if they haven't got any business."

"Who cares about Elan?" Heather declared coldly. "There are other modeling agencies—like the one Roger Harlan wants to sign with."

"Really?" said Nancy, taking in this bit of information.

"And there are other clothing companies, too," Heather added, her voice dropping darkly. "Big ones. Bigger than Smash!"

"Like Let's Go?" Nancy said.

"Bigger than that. Now I have to go," Heather snapped, getting up and walking away.

"Things are starting to fall into place now,"

Nancy told Kelly. "Let's get back to the hotel. Everybody will be gathering there before long. I want to ask Monique Durand about those go-sees."

"I'll meet you there later," Kelly said. "But, Nancy, shouldn't we be tailing Heather?"

"I don't think so," Nancy said.

"You mean Heather's not the one we're after?" Kelly gasped.

"Maybe, maybe not," Nancy said. "But I'll tell you one thing—she's not the *only* one."

In the hotel lobby Nancy watched as workers carried in large blowups of the contestants' pictures.

"Hi." Nancy nodded to one of the workers who was busy hanging up a blowup of Bess. "Hi." The worker nodded back, then called across the room to a colleague. "Is this number three, Eddie?"

Eddie consulted a large sheet of paper. "Right," he confirmed. "Hang it there."

Nancy stepped back to admire Bess's picture. She was smiling pertly into the camera, and though her expression was a little stiff, she looked good. Leo Halsey wasn't a bad photographer, but he was no genius either.

Maggie Adams's photo was sheer magic,

though. Her smile lit up her whole face, and the overall effect of the photo was relaxed and natural. Nancy couldn't help gazing at Maggie's picture a little longer than she did at the others.

When Heather's pictures were placed on the wall, Nancy did a double take. How could someone so cold and devoid of charm be so lovely and sincere-looking in a photo? Obviously Heather had genuine ability at modeling.

"The candids go over here, right, Eddie?" Again Eddie consulted his paper. "Yeah, but be sure to go by the numbers. The art director wants them in a specific order."

Nancy looked around for Monique Durand, but Elan's owner still hadn't shown up, so she sauntered over to the candids for a quick peek. There were Carey Harper and Diana Amsterdam letting off steam by jumping on their beds. There was Alison Williams sharing a tender moment with her date from the banquet, Elan model Daryl Hancock. There were Trudy Woo and Natasha going crazy over dresses in a boutique.

"I only got nine here, Eddie," the worker told his colleague after he'd hung several photos.

"That's funny. Let me check the list," Eddie said. "Okay, one is missing, you're right," he announced. "The one that was taken before the big disaster at the fountain."

Before the big disaster? Nancy felt her heart quicken. Why was that particular photo missing? And just what did it show?

Maybe if somebody had taken the trouble to steal it, the photo might hold the key to the entire mystery!

Eddie scratched his head. "I don't get it," he said. "Everything else is here."

The picture may have shown the culprit setting up the paint-spraying contraption, Nancy thought.

"Here's the guy who can tell us where it is," Eddie said.

Nancy turned her head and saw Bogorofsky walk in. "Hello, everyone," he said. "I come to look at the results."

"Mr. Bogorofsky, we're missing one of the candids you took at the fountain," Eddie said. Bogorofsky shook his head in disgust. "I can't print another. The negatives are missing. The second robbery I've had this week! This is ridiculous!"

Nancy had heard enough, so she made for the exit.

She raced through the lobby and hopped into a cab. The sooner she reached Kelly, the better.

Kelly had taken all sorts of candid shots for *Teen Scene* on the day of the fountain shoot. If they were lucky, one of those shots would reveal the same secret as the missing photo.

"I need your help, Kelly," Nancy told her at the *Teen Scene* offices. "Those candids you took at Buckingham Fountain?"

"What about them?" Kelly asked.

Nancy explained about the missing photo while Kelly started searching through her drawers. "They were right here," the reporter murmured.

Nancy held her breath. Was it possible the culprit had gotten there first?

"Eureka!" At last Kelly pulled out a large manila envelope marked "Face of the Year." "I don't know if you'll find anything here, though," she confessed. "All I have are shots of the girls standing around before the shoot. After that purple stuff came out of the fountain I didn't take any more."

"That's just what I'm looking for." Kelly opened the envelope and spread the proof sheets out. Each eight-by-ten sheet contained thirty-two one-inch pictures.

"Here, Nancy," Kelly said, pulling a magnifying glass from her top drawer. "You'll need this."

Nancy peered through the glass at the tiny black and white glossies. There was Alison joking around with Bess and Natasha. There was

Bogorofsky yelling at one of the lighting men. There was Heather stepping to the front pedestal. And behind her, in the back of the fountain . . .

"There! See that?" Nancy said, taking a pencil and pointing to the corner of the photo.

"What is that, a bush?" Kelly asked.

Nancy handed Kelly the magnifying glass.

"It's a person!" Kelly exclaimed.

"He's crouching behind the fountain," Nancy added. "Right where I found the paint can."

"But who could it be?" Kelly looked up from the photo.

Nancy's heart soared in triumph. "Who wears a coat with a fur collar?" she asked, even though she knew the answer. "Nobody from the lighting crew, that's for sure."

The answer hit Kelly just as Nancy said it out loud.

"Thom Fortner!"

Chapter

Fifteen

KELLY STARED AT NANCY in total shock. "You're absolutely right," Kelly said. "That is his coat."

"Don't you see, Kelly? It makes perfect sense!" Nancy picked up the proof sheet and sank down on a director's chair. "Thom Fortner had the opportunity to do a lot of damage during this contest," she murmured.

"He even had access to the beauty salon," Kelly noted.

"The sawed-through railing, the broken ring at

the exercise station," Nancy went on. "He was at all those places."

"But why would Thom Fortner want to sabotage his own project?" Kelly asked. "It doesn't make sense! The Face of the Year contest is big business, and it's his baby."

Nancy put a hand on her face and rubbed her eyes. An image flashed into her mind of Thom Fortner riding the escalator at Marshall Field's with a woman—a woman who looked familiar. . . .

Opening her eyes wide, Nancy exclaimed, "I know the answer to that question, Kelly! And her name is Trina Evans!"

"Trina Evans, the head of Let's Go?" Kelly's eyes widened.

"Remember the note Thom dropped?" Nancy asked. "It was signed *T,* and it mentioned a 'new president.' That note was from Trina Evans— she's his new president!"

"Wow," said Kelly, leaning back in her chair to take it all in.

"I even saw them together," Nancy said.

"I read an article where Trina blasted the Face of the Year contest," Kelly tossed in.

"Right! Because it looked like it was going to be a major success for Smash. But Trina must have decided to get someone inside the contest to sabotage it—someone like Thom Fortner. Then the whole contest would backfire on Smash."

Nancy stood up and pressed her lips together. "Kelly," she said, "lock up these proof sheets and the negatives. They're our best bit of hard evidence."

"They won't go anywhere, don't worry. Hey!" Kelly exclaimed, glancing at her watch and standing up. "Speaking of Smash, I've got to be over there in ten minutes to vote," she said.

"See you tonight, then," Nancy said. "It's going to be quite an evening, if I'm not mistaken."

Nancy hurried back to the hotel, where she ran into Bess in the lobby.

"Just think, Nancy," Bess said excitedly. "At this very moment the judges are all up at Smash voting for Face of the Year. I can hardly wait till tonight!"

"Bess," Nancy replied, lightly grasping her friend by the arm, "come on up to our room. I want to tell you something."

"You've solved the case! Tell me, tell me!"

Nancy waited until they were in their suite with the door closed before she told Bess her theory about Thom's motive for sabotaging the contest.

"It sounds good, Nancy," Bess admitted. "But like you always say, where's the proof? The note he dropped isn't much evidence. And you said you couldn't see his face in those pictures."

"Right, but I think I know where we might be able to find a lot more," Nancy said slowly. "Do you know where I can find Heather?"

"Heather!" Bess exclaimed in surprise. "I forgot all about her. She should be in her room. We were all told to be back at the hotel."

"Thanks, Bess." Nancy headed for the door.

"Nan, be careful," Bess said.

"I'm always careful," Nancy promised, slipping out and heading for Heather's room.

"Hello?" Heather called out in response to Nancy's knock.

"It's Nancy Drew. Can I come in for a minute?"

Heather pulled the door open. "I'm getting ready for tonight," she said.

"I won't take a lot of your time," Nancy promised. "But I need Thom Fortner's briefcase. And I want you to help me get it."

"What do you want Thom's briefcase for? And why should I help you?" Heather flopped into a chair.

"I think you'll want to, when you know what's in it for you."

145

Intrigued, Heather arched one of her perfectly shaped eyebrows. "Go on," she said.

"If you help, and if *Teen Scene* breaks the story of what was really going on in this contest, you'll get some great publicity—enough publicity to bury your past for good."

Heather took Nancy in with her catlike golden eyes. "What if *Teen Scene* doesn't break the story?"

"Kelly Conroy is helping me investigate," Nancy said. "She'll break the story. I promise."

Heather appeared thoughtful before speaking. "Forget it," she said. "I don't want anybody mad at me."

"Suit yourself," said Nancy, stepping to the door. "But if you change your mind, look me up. I'll be in the audience tonight."

"Nancy!" Bess said excitedly when Nancy went back to her room. "Call Kelly right away. She's waiting at a pay phone."

"Hi," came Kelly's voice. Sounds of the street filtered into the phone.

"What's up?" Nancy asked.

"I was just up at Smash for the voting," Kelly explained. "Me, Thom, Bettina, Monique, Roger Harlan—"

"And?" Nancy asked.

"And when we were finished, Thom counted

the votes and announced that Heather Richards had won."

"Oh," said Nancy, a little deflated.

"But," Kelly added, "when Thom put the votes into his briefcase, I could swear he was trying to hide something. Everybody left, including me, but I had a funny feeling about the results. I sneaked back inside. The pads we had written on were still on the table."

"And?" Nancy asked.

"And, Nancy, I could read the indentations on the pads. I could read who everyone had voted for. And guess what? Heather didn't win at all!"

Chapter

Sixteen

LISTEN, KELLY, did anyone see what you did?" Nancy asked anxiously.

"I don't think so."

"Good. I think there's something we can do about this. *Tonight,*" Nancy stressed. "Meet me in my room before the ceremony so we can go over what to do next. And keep those pads— they're hard evidence!"

"Well, Nancy, how do I look?" Bess stepped away from the mirror and spun around for

Nancy's benefit. The soft pink dress, off one shoulder, was perfect on her.

"Bess, you look fabulous," Nancy told her.

"Oh, if I win this contest I'll be the happiest girl in the entire universe!" Bess promised.

A knock on the door interrupted her. "Bess?" Maggie called from the other side. "Are you ready?"

"As ready as I can be," Bess said with a giggle, pulling the door open. "Come on, Nancy."

"You go on ahead," Nancy said. "Kelly's stopping by for me."

"Okay," Bess said. She practically floated out of the suite.

Nancy waited only a few minutes before Kelly showed up. "Good. You're here," Nancy said. "Now here's the plan. We're going to put on a little performance of our own tonight—and you're going to steal the show."

Thom Fortner stood up from the table where he was sitting with the other judges. He walked over to the podium, followed by Kelly, who handed him a sealed envelope. "All right, ladies and gentlemen," he announced. "This is the moment we've all been waiting for."

"Nobody more than me, Thom," Nancy murmured under her breath. "Nobody more than me."

Thom signaled the band leader, and the drummer began a low drumroll. Up on the stage behind Thom and Kelly sat the eight contestants. All the girls sat open-eyed, waiting for the announcement that could change their lives. Heather already wore a triumphant grin.

"This afternoon," Thom said as the drum rolled under his voice, "the judges faced a terrible task. They had to choose just one young lady out of these eight very special contestants to be the Face of the Year. And the young lady that they chose is"—he ripped open the envelope—"Ms.—"

Kelly Conroy reached out, snatched the paper from Thom's hand, looked at it, and, before Thom could react, shouted, "Maggie Adams!"

The audience erupted into a huge cheer, the band broke into a jubilant song, and Maggie rose to her feet, beaming. Nancy noticed that Monique was clapping especially hard.

Heather flew out of her chair and screeched at Thom, "You liar!" She shook her fist. "This whole contest is a sham! I was supposed to win! You promised!"

"Why did he promise you you'd win, Heather?" Nancy called from her place near the front.

"Stop this! Stop this, please!" Monique stood up and threw her napkin down while Bettina covered her mouth to mask her laugh.

"Because he wanted to shut me up. I saw him cut the railing on the pier. I also know that Trina Evans is hiring him. He's leaving Smash to work for Let's Go the minute this contest is over."

Shocked, Monique turned to Thom. "Is this true, Thom?" she gasped. Then she said, "Don't say a word. I can see by your face that it is. How could you?" The owner of Elan, the most powerful starmaker in the modeling world, sank back in her chair and cried like a little girl. Next to her, Bettina sat, stunned.

The press was having a field day. Flashes went off all around.

Thom Fortner, who'd been standing with his mouth hanging open, finally recovered. "She's lying!" he shouted, pointing at Heather.

"Then why don't you show us what's in your briefcase, Thom?" Nancy called out. Silence fell as all eyes turned toward the public relations director.

"Young lady, you are not a part of this contest! Get her out of here!" Thom shouted.

"She's my friend! I invited her here!" Bess cried. "You know, I bet you're the creep who wrote her that threatening note!"

"He also planted Roger Harlan's tie tack at the scene of the first accident to make it look like Roger was sabotaging the contest," Nancy added.

"What nonsense!" Thom reacted with a bitter laugh. "You have no proof, none at all!" He reached under the podium for his briefcase. Before he could grab it, though, a fist crashed into his jaw.

"That's for trying to implicate me," snarled Roger Harlan. He grabbed the briefcase and tossed it to Nancy. Inside was everything Nancy needed to back up her accusation of Thom. The passkey was there, the photo of Thom tampering with the fountain, and the original ballots proclaiming Maggie the winner. A defeated Thom Fortner stood rubbing his jaw.

"I think you'd better find yourself a good attorney," Nancy told him. "You may be in for the Lawsuit of the Year."

"I'm so happy for you," Bess said to Maggie the next morning. She and Nancy were standing in the lobby, waiting for Nancy's car to be brought out front.

"I only wish we all could have won," Maggie said, smiling warmly at Bess.

Roger Harlan walked over to the three girls. "Next time you're in Chicago, look me up," he told Bess and Nancy. Then he looked at Maggie. Nancy could feel the electricity that crackled between them. "I hope I'll be seeing more of you, too," he added softly. Maggie glowed.

"Well, I'm sure we'll see both of your faces all the time," said Bess. "And if you're in New York or Paris or Rome, we just might look you up there!"

"Your car, miss." The doorman tapped Nancy on the shoulder.

"This is really goodbye," Nancy said, giving Maggie a quick hug and reaching out to shake Roger's hand. "Come on, Bess."

Bess waved to Maggie and started walking to the door. "It's funny. I just met them a few days ago, but I'm really going to miss them."

Nancy and Bess stepped to the car as a hotel employee handed Nancy her keys.

A porter who'd carried their bags to the car banged the trunk lid shut. "You're all set," he said.

Nancy thanked him and pulled the car out of the driveway.

"Oh, well, that's the end of that," Bess said, taking something out of her handbag and unwrapping it. "Want a Danish, Nancy? I have two. I got them from the hotel dining room this morning."

Nancy glanced at the pastry in her friend's hand. "Maybe later," she said. "I'm still stuffed from breakfast."

"I figured, why let good food go to waste?" Bess said, opening her mouth to take a big bite.

"You mean the food will go to *your* waist, don't you?" Nancy asked with a twinkle in her eye.

"Oh, be quiet," Bess said. "You know, Nancy, I'm glad I didn't win that contest."

Nancy's jaw dropped open. "I can't believe my ears! You are?"

Bess swallowed another bite of Danish. "Yes. Do you realize the pressure a model is under? She always has to look good. If she gets a pimple or gains five pounds, it's an absolute disaster! I mean, the whole world of modeling is so fake! A person like Heather can come off really beautiful just because of lighting and makeup, and—"

"And perfect features and a devastating figure," Nancy finished for her with a smile.

"True, she does have those," Bess said. "But she's not really beautiful. Not like Maggie. Not inside, where it counts.

"I really learned a lot this week, Nancy. I mean, Maggie may be the Face of the Year," Bess said, "but you're the detective of the decade—and the best friend of the century!"

Nancy's next case:

The exciting world of law enforcement is the subject of a high school career fair, and Nancy is a guest speaker. But the real excitement begins when speaker Tom Hayward, head of a fast-growing security company, takes center stage. He gets an urgent message that a warehouse he protects has just been robbed!

The theft is just one in a series of burglaries plaguing Hayward Security, and Nancy suspects that someone has set the company up to take a fall. But as she closes in on the truth, Nancy finds that she, too, is being set up. If she doesn't catch the rip-off artist fast, he might just paint her out of the picture for good . . . in *DANGER FOR HIRE*, Case #52 in The Nancy Drew Files™.